DAWN AND THE SURFER GHOST

Over the next week, the kids at the beach programme were full of speculation about the surfer ghost. The story grew, and soon other people were reporting sightings. Even at school, it was all anybody talked about. I think a lot of people were just having fun with the story, but I took it seriously. I *knew* I'd seen something that night. It *looked* like a ghost. And if it was a surfing ghost, it could have been the ghost of Thrash. His spirit might be haunting our beach. This could be the best ghost story yet!

Also available in the Babysitters Club Mysteries series:

Look out for:

DAWN AND THE
SURFER GHOST

Ann M. Martin

Hippo

The author gratefully acknowledges
Ellen Miles
for her help in preparing this manuscript.

Scholastic Children's Books,
7-9 Pratt Street, London NW1 0AE, UK
a division of Scholastic Publications Ltd
London ~ New York ~ Toronto ~ Sydney ~ Auckland

First published in the US by Scholastic Inc., 1993
First published in the UK by Scholastic Publications Ltd, 1995

Text copyright © Ann M. Martin, 1993
THE BABYSITTERS CLUB is a registered trademark of Scholastic Inc.

ISBN 0 590 13268 7

Typeset in Plantin by Contour Typesetters, Southall, London
Printed by Cox & Wyman Ltd, Reading, Berks

10 9 8 7 6 5 4 3 2 1

1st CHAPTER

Saturday

Dear Mary Anne,
   How are you? I'm fine-and very busy. I miss you like crazy! Thanks for your letter I got it yesterday. It's good to hear all about what's going on in Stoneybrook. I miss Stoneybrook like crazy, too, believe it or not. And of course, I miss the BSC. I sure wish I could be at the sleepover at Stacey's tonight. Oh, well. Even though I miss everything and everyone back in Connecticut, I'm having a great time here in California. It's wonderful to be with

1

Dad and Jeff and my old friends. If only there were some way I could live in both places at once, life would be perfect! Anyway, I have a lot to tell you, but it'll have to wait. Right now I'm late for my surfing lesson! Can you believe it? I'm actually taking surfing lessons. More about that soon. Give my love to Richard, and give my mum a big hug for me, okay? Love always, your sister and best friend—

Dawn

Just as I signed my name, my dad called from the kitchen, "Dawn! Your lift's here!"

"Thanks!" I called back. I folded the letter I'd just dashed off, addressed an envelope, stuck on a stamp, grabbed my beach bag and left my room. I was going to drop the letter into a letterbox on the way to the beach. I walked down the long, tiled hall leading to the kitchen. My father was standing by the sink, drinking a glass of carrot juice he'd just whipped up. "'Bye, Dad," I said, giving him a hug.

"See you later, Sunshine," he said, hugging me back. (Sunshine's his baby name for me. Ugh!) "Be careful, okay?"

"I will," I said. "Don't worry." Just

then, I heard a car horn sound outside, and I knew that my friend's mum was getting impatient. "See you!" I called, as I ran out of the door.

"Sorry, Mrs Winslow," I said when I was settled in the back seat of the car.

"Oh, that's all right," she replied. "Actually, Sunny was the one who sounded the horn. She can't wait to get to the beach."

Sunny, who was sitting in the front seat, turned to face me. She grinned. "Surf's up, you know!" she exclaimed.

"Cowabunga!" I said, grinning in return. Then I buckled my seat-belt, leaned back, and relaxed. It was a beautiful midwinter day in California, the "Golden State", and I was on my way to the beach. What could be better?

I suppose I ought to stop here and introduce myself. My name's Dawn Schafer, and I'm thirteen years old and in the eighth grade. I've got long blonde hair and blue eyes. I suppose my life might seem a little confusing to anybody else, but to me it makes sense. Let's see, how can I explain everything? Perhaps I'll practise something I've been learning in English, and make an outline. Have you ever been asked to do that? You know, with roman numerals and letters and everything? It's not easy, but it can be a good way to sort out a lot of information. So, here goes:

I. Sharon Porter, my mother, is born in Stoneybrook, Connecticut.
   A. Grows up.
   B. Has high-school sweetheart, Richard Spier, but does not marry him.
   C. Moves to California, and marries Jack Schafer.
   D. Has two children, Dawn (that's me) and Jeff (my younger brother).

II. My parents get a divorce.
   A. My mother, Jeff and I move back to Stoneybrook.
   B. My father stays in California.
   C. I make good friends and join a special babysitting club (the BSC).
   D. Jeff is unhappy in Connecticut, and moves back to live with my father.

III. Mary Anne Spier (my new best friend) and I find out that her father (a widower) and my mum were those high-school sweethearts I mentioned before.
   A. We get them together and they start dating again.
   B. They (surprise!) fall in love.

IV. My mother remarries.
   A. My new best friend becomes my sister.
   B. We all live happily in our old Connecticut farmhouse.

4

V. I really, really miss my dad, Jeff and California.
   A. I decide to go back to California for a few months.
   B. Here I am!

Phew! Pretty complicated, right? Just be glad I didn't put in all the other things, which would have been listed under the As and Bs as 1s, 2s and 3s. I could even have put in 1as, bs and cs. But that would have made the outline about ten pages long. Anyway, I think you get the idea.

Being back in California has been really cool. I love hanging around with my friend Sunny Winslow. She and I have been friends for years, so we've got a special kind of bond. And after she heard about the babysitting club I belong to in Stoneybrook, she started one here. They welcomed me as a temporary member, which means I'm still able to do one of my favourite things: look after little kids.

Being in California also means spending more time with my dad and Jeff, which makes me very happy. Jeff's ten now, and I think that's a really fun age. I even like Mrs Bruen, the housekeeper Dad hired when Jeff moved back in with him. She keeps the house spotless and cooks us terrific meals. The only thing about California that I'm not crazy about is Carol Olson. She's this woman my dad has been seeing for a while, and while I don't exactly *dislike* her, I don't love her, either. Actually, I'd probably like her all right if she didn't happen to be my dad's girlfriend. I mean, she's young and pretty and drives a little red sports car, and she likes MTV. She's cool, in other words. Which is fine for an ordinary person, but not really so fine for a woman my *father* might be serious about. Do you know what I mean? Anyway, Jeff and I have learned to get on with Carol and accept that she's in our lives at the moment, but that's as far as I go.

There's actually one other bad thing about California, but I've already mentioned it. It's how much I miss Stoneybrook and the people who live there, especially Mary Anne and my mum. Mary Anne's my best friend in the world, even though I haven't known her nearly as long as I've known Sunny. And my mum? My mum's a wonderful person. She may not be as organized as my dad or as neat as Mrs Bruen (in fact, she's a completely *dis*organized slob), but she's funny and bright and very loving and—and I'd better not think about her any more just now or I might start feeling really sad.

And who wants to be sad when she's about to hit the beach? I was excited about going surfing that day, and nothing could ruin my mood. Sunny and I started going to surfing lessons not long ago, when we heard that a big surfing competition was coming up. Practically all the kids at school are planning to enter at least one event, and everybody's busy preparing for it. I haven't surfed for ages, and I was never all that good at it when I *did* do it, but I thought being involved in the competition would be a nice way to feel that I fit in with my old California friends. As it turned out, this time around I just *loved* surfing. I wouldn't have kept it up if I didn't, as "fitting in" isn't as important to me as being happy with myself. Anyway, surfing's great! There's nothing like the feeling you get when you're out in the ocean, just you and your board and the waves. I can't explain it any better than that, but trust me, it's wonderful.

Sunny's been enjoying herself, too, although I think she may be enjoying the surfer *guys* more than surfing itself. She loves hanging around on the beach or in the surf shop and chatting to all the incredibly cute, tanned boys. Those guys practically *live* on the beach. Surfing's everything to them, and even a pretty, bright girl like Sunny doesn't always distract them from watching for the perfect wave. This is frustrating for Sunny, I think. But she has a good time, anyway. And even though she doesn't pay as much attention as I do during our lessons, she seems to have a knack for the sport.

"Have fun, girls," said Mrs Winslow. We'd arrived at the beach, and Sunny and I had jumped out of the car. "I'll pick you up here in three hours," Sunny's mum went on. "Be careful!"

"We will!" we chorused.

"Thanks for the ride," I added.

"Come on," said Sunny, as her mum drove off. "We have to go and hire our boards before all the good ones have gone."

"I'm coming," I replied. But I wasn't in a rush. First I wanted to drink in the sights and sounds of the beach. I still wasn't used to the idea that I could come here any time (any time I could get a lift, that is; the beach isn't exactly walking distance from my dad's house) and enjoy the warm sun, the hot sand, the blue ocean crested with white and the seagulls that fly overhead, crying just loudly enough to be heard over the surf. I can sit on the beach and look and listen for hours. To me, it's the most beautiful place in the world. I think beaches kind of get in your blood, and if you grow up near one you never feel quite right when you're away from it.

Oh, there are beaches in Connecticut, all right. But they're not the same. The beaches on the West Coast are bigger, the surf's higher and the sun's brighter. And there's nothing like sunset over the Pacific.

"Dawn, come *on*," said Sunny, grabbing my arm and practically *dragging* me towards the surf shop. The little building was crowded with surfers, but we fought our way through them and chose the boards we wanted to hire. As we were standing in the queue to pay for them, Sunny leaned over to whisper in my ear. "Don't look now, but that's Thrash back there, working on that board."

I glanced into the back of the shop where a guy was working on a surfboard laid across two saw-horses. I couldn't get a good look at him, but I could tell he was a little older than most of the high-school kids who usually hang around at the shop. "Who's Thrash?" I whispered back.

"Only the hottest surfer around," said Sunny. "He's incredible. I've seen him do some really radical stuff out there." She nodded towards the waves.

"Well, maybe if we practise hard, we'll be that good one day, too," I said. We'd reached the front of the line, and we paid for our hire boards. "Ready for our lesson?" I asked Sunny. We were supposed to meet Buck, our instructor, on the beach, so we grabbed our boards and ran for it.

The waves were perfect that day, and I

surfed better than I ever had before. By the time I got back home I felt exhausted, but it was a good kind of tired. I had just enough energy to help Jeff with his maths homework. Then, after a dinner of nachos with guacamole (I made it, as Mrs Bruen doesn't work on Saturdays), I settled down on the living room sofa and rang my friend Stacey McGill's number. I knew from Mary Anne's letter that my friends in the BSC would be at her house for a sleepover, and I was dying to hear their voices.

Stacey answered, and I talked to her for a few minutes. Then I talked to Mary Anne and to my other friends: Kristy Thomas, Claudia Kishi, Jessi Ramsey and Shannon Kilbourne. The only member of the BSC I didn't talk to was Mallory Pike, because she's getting over ME and she isn't allowed to go to sleepovers. They told me the latest Stoneybrook news, and I told them about surfing. It was great to hear their voices. I miss them so much, and I know they miss me, too. Like I said, life would be perfect if only I could live in two places at once. But the next best thing is to feel at home in both places, and to know that the friends I've made are friends for ever.

2nd CHAPTER

Monday

Dear Everybody,
   I'm just about to go to a
meeting of the We ♥ Kids
Club, so of course I'm thinking
about all of you in the BSC.
You're meeting today, too, I
know. Claudia is probably
passing around Ring-Dings,
Kristy is sitting in her director's
chair, and the rest of you
are most likely chatting about
the latest adventures of
Jackie Rodowsky, the Walking
Disaster. I wish I could be
there with you. Not that I'm

craving a Ring-Ding or anything, because I still hate junk food. (Sorry, Claud!) It's just that I miss you all a whole lot. Take Care!

WBS, Dawn

In case you don't know, WBS stands for Write Back Soon. I didn't really have to add that, as I get letters all the time from Mary Anne and the rest of my friends in the BSC. But those letters mean a lot to me, and I want to keep them coming. I sealed the envelope, addressed it and stuck a few funny stickers on the back. Then I headed for Sunny's house for a meeting of the We ♥ Kids Club, which is the babysitting club Sunny started.

Sunny lives just down the road from my dad's house, so it didn't take long to walk there. When I arrived, the other members of the club were already there. Sunny had made a snack for the meeting, and everybody was digging in.

I sat down next to Maggie Blume, one of the club members. "Hi, Dawn," she said, passing me a bag of organic corn chips. "Try the spinach dip—it's great."

"It's even better with the vegetables," said Jill Henderson, holding up a piece of raw broccoli dripping with green and white dip.

12

Sunny passed me the plate of vegetables. "Help yourself," she said.

I took a piece of carrot and dunked it. This kind of snack is one of the reasons I like the We ♥ Kids Club. My friends and I like healthy, nutritious food—no Hula Hoops for us! During BSC meetings, I always felt a little out of it when I turned down Claudia's offerings of junk food, but here I fit right in.

Don't get me wrong. It's not as if *everybody* in California's a health-food nut. Plenty of people here think that big, greasy tacos or hamburgers and chips are perfect foods. But I was brought up on mostly healthy, organic food (so were my friends here), and it just tastes better to me.

Anyway, as I mentioned, Sunny started the We ♥ Kids Club after I told her about the BSC. The California club is modelled on the Connecticut club. They're not identical, though—in fact, they're not even close. The BSC's more like a business than a club. It has officers, for one thing. Kristy Thomas, the chairman, is the one who came up with the idea for it. She thought it would be great if parents could reach a lot of sitters with one phone call, and she was right. The club meets three days a week: Mondays, Wednesdays and Fridays from five-thirty till six. That's when parents can phone to book sitters. The BSC's got seven members—most of the time, that is. Lately the club's been changing a bit.

Kristy's a real go-getter. She's the one who thinks up most of the ideas for the club. For example, the club record book, in which we keep track of our appointments. Also, the club notebook, in which we write up our babysitting experiences so the other club members can read them and stay informed about our clients. Kristy also invented Kid-Kits, which are boxes full of games, toys and other things that kids love. They're great for rainy-day sitting jobs.

Kristy's got brown hair and eyes, and she loves sport. She's got a big family: her mum, two older brothers and one younger one, a stepfather, a stepbrother, a stepsister, an adopted baby sister and a grandmother who lives with the family. Also a dog, a cat and two goldfish!

The vice-chairman of the BSC is Claudia Kishi. The club meets in her room and uses her private phone line. Claudia's Japanese-American, and she's drop-dead gorgeous, with long black hair and almond-shaped eyes. As I've told you, she loves junk food. She also loves Nancy Drew mysteries, shopping, boys and art. Especially art. Claudia's a very talented artist, and her creativity shows in the wild way she dresses. Unlike her older sister, who's a certified genius, Claudia's not a particularly good student. Her parents wish she would "apply herself", but they're very understanding and supportive about her love for art.

My best friend (and sister!) Mary Anne is the secretary of the BSC. She keeps track of all our scheduling, and she does a great job. Mary Anne's shy, quiet and sensitive. She's got a boyfriend, and a kitten named Tigger. Her mum died when Mary Anne was a little girl, and her father (who's now my stepfather) was a very strict parent until recently. Luckily, he's loosened up a lot, and now Mary Anne's treated more like a teenager and less like a little girl. Mary Anne's not only *my* best friend, but Kristy's, too. She and Kristy look rather alike, as Mary Anne also has brown eyes and hair, and is quite short. But Mary Anne had her hair cut in a cool new style recently, and now she looks trendier than Kristy.

The treasurer of the BSC is Stacey McGill. She's a whiz at maths, so keeping track of our money is easy for her. She collects subs every Monday, which we use for things like paying Claudia's phone bill and buying supplies for our Kid-Kits. Stacey grew up in New York City, and she's pretty sophisticated. She's got fluffy blonde hair which she perms, and she dresses *very* stylishly. Stacey's parents got divorced not long ago, and her dad still lives in New

York. Luckily for the BSC, Stacey chose to live in Stoneybrook with her mum. Stacey's diabetic, which means that her body doesn't process sugar correctly. She really has to watch what she eats; in fact, she's the only other member of the BSC who turns down Claudia's junk food!

Jessi Ramsey and Mallory Pike aren't officers; they're junior members of the BSC. Unlike the rest of the members, who are thirteen and in the eighth grade, Jessi and Mal are eleven and in the sixth grade. They aren't allowed to sit alone at night, so they take a lot of afternoon jobs. Jessi's African-American, and she's got a little sister and a baby brother. Her great-aunt lives with the family, to help out with the kids, as both of Jessi's parents work. Jessi's a very talented ballet student, and she's got the long legs of a ballerina. Mallory, who isn't coming to BSC meetings these days because of her ME, comes from a huge family of eight kids! She's the oldest, so she's used to babysitting. Mal's got curly red hair, glasses and a brace. She's in an awkward phase just now, but I think she's going to be really pretty in a few years.

The BSC also has an associate member who doesn't necessarily come to meetings, but is available if we need an extra sitter. His name's Logan Bruno, and he's Mary

Anne's boyfriend. He's from Kentucky, and he's got the most luscious Southern accent.

My BSC job, when I'm in Connecticut, is to be the alternate officer. That means I can fill in for anyone who's absent. The BSC has temporarily replaced me with Shannon Kilbourne, a girl from the neighbourhood Kristy moved to when her mother remarried. Shannon's usually an associate member, but now that I'm away, she's more like a full-time member.

Anyway, as I said, the We ♥ Kids Club is very different from the BSC, and the snacks aren't the only example of this. The We ♥ Kids Club has no officers, no club notebook and no regular meetings. The members just get together whenever they feel like it. Clients can call any time, and whoever wants a job takes it. It seems to work out okay, even though it's much less organized than the BSC. The We ♥ Kids Club has one thing that the BSC *doesn't* have: a cookbook full of healthy recipes. The club members also have recipe files that they update. The kids they sit for love to spend time in the kitchen, cooking up Granola Snack Squares, Veggi Bursts and other fun, nutritious treats.

Sunny's the only member of the club I know well. She and I have always got along like sisters, maybe because we've spent so much time together. Sunny's mum is like a second mother to me. Mrs Winslow's really great; she's a potter, and makes amazing things out of clay. She and her husband used to be hippies, I think. Sunny's real name is Sunshine Daydream, if you can believe that! (It's just a coincidence that my dad calls me Sunshine, but Sunny and I always thought that made us soul sisters.) Sunny's got blonde hair, but she's not a stereotypical Californian, and none of the other members are, either. Sunny's hair's strawberry-blonde, with lots of red high-lights, and she's got freckles across her upturned nose. She always seems to be in a good mood, and she loves flirting. One thing that Sunny and I have in common is that we love ghost stories. She's got loads of great books, and we like to swap them with each other. And nobody can beat Sunny for telling a scary story when the lights are out during a sleepover.

Maggie Blume lives a few blocks away from Sunny and me. Her dad's involved in the movies, but Maggie never acts stuck up about it. Once in a while she'll mention that "Tom" or "Winona" came to dinner the night before, but she won't make a big point of saying that it was Tom Cruise or Winona Ryder. Maggie's got a little brother called Zeke, who's been in a few advertisements. The Blumes' house is huge and sprawling, and they've got a swimming pool that looks like a tropical lagoon. I suppose they must be rich.

Maggie's got very short hair, cut in a punky style with a long tail hanging down the back. Sometimes her mum lets her dye a red or purple or pink streak in it. Her hair goes with her clothes, which are pretty wild. She likes wearing big black boots, and leather jackets over vintage dresses (from the 1950s). Maggie likes really loud rock music. But she's not a punk or anything. She's a very nice girl, and a good student. She happens to love ghost stories, too, almost as much as Sunny and I do.

Jill Henderson's got dark blonde hair, almost brown, and deep brown eyes that remind me of chocolate. She's quiet and self-assured, and rather serious. Jill lives in a small house in the hills with her mother, who's divorced, and her older sister Liz. The Hendersons have got three dogs that they love dearly. Their names are Spike, Shakespeare and Smee, and they're all boxers with funny, ugly faces.

That day at our meeting, Jill was telling us how Smee likes chasing the cat next door.

"It makes Mrs Banks angry," she said, "so I try to keep him away from her precious Tinkerbell. But once in a while he gets away from me, and you should see how they run through the bushes! I actually think Tinkerbell enjoys being chased, but there's no way I can convince Mrs Banks of that." Jill grinned.

Just then the phone rang, and Sunny answered it. "Hold on," she said, after listening for a moment. She put her hand over the receiver. "Who wants to sit for Clover and Daffodil next Tuesday at eight?" she asked.

"I will!" I said. Clover and Daffodil are the two girls who live next door to me. They're lots of fun to sit for.

Sunny arranged the job and rang off. "Dawn, you and I had better be careful about taking too many jobs," she said. "We're going to be pretty busy with the children's programme."

"I know," I said. "But Clover and Daffodil are no trouble. And I'll be back from the beach in plenty of time." Sunny and I had just got involved in a special children's programme at the beach. It takes place on Tuesday, Wednesday and Thursday afternoons, and most Saturdays, and it's mainly for kids with working parents. The programme's a lot of fun, and it's perfect for us, because a bus takes the kids— and us—to the beach straight from school. That way, we don't have to worry about getting lifts to the beach for surfing lessons. (We have some time to ourselves when we've finished helping with the kids.) I'm enjoying getting to know the kids. Actually, I already knew three of them. One, Stephie Robertson, is an eight-year-old girl with asthma, and the other two are brothers called Erick and Ryan DeWitt, who are real terrors. Erick's eight and Ryan's six, and together they can be really devilish.

"We'll have to make sure we separate Erick and Ryan tomorrow," said Sunny. "They behave much better when they're not acting as a team."

"Good idea," I said, remembering a sand-throwing fight they'd started last week. I dunked another piece of broccoli into the dip and smiled. The We ♥ Kids Club might be different from the BSC, but the members of both clubs share one important quality: they understand kids and love babysitting. I felt quite at home.

3rd
CHAPTER

Tuesday

Dear Stacey,
    Remember how much you
liked surfing when the
BSC took a holiday out here?
Now I know just how you
felt. I wasn't crazy about
surfing before, but now I'm
addicted to it. I wish you
could be here with me, riding
those waves!

More later—

I'd been thinking of Stacey a lot lately, ever since I found out how much fun surfing could be. I remembered when my friends in the BSC came to California, after we won a lottery. That was when I lived full-time in Stoneybrook. Everybody had a great time, and Stacey spent nearly the whole holiday on the beach, learning to surf.

I'd started that letter to Stacey during a study period. I should have been studying for an English test, but I was having a hard time concentrating. That day, after school, Sunny and I would be going to the beach to help with the children's programme. And afterwards, we'd planned to practise our surfing. I could hardly wait.

When the last bell rang, I ran out to the courtyard to meet Sunny. I sat on a bench in the sun as I waited, and thought how different my California school is from Stoneybrook Middle School, the school my friends back in Connecticut were attending that same day.

SMS is a perfectly nice school. It's an old brick building with wide corridors and big windows in each classroom. But my school in California's totally different. It's a series of one-storey buildings arranged in a star shape around a big courtyard. There are skylights in all the classrooms, so the rooms are flooded with light. The courtyard is full of plants and trees, and it looks like a tropical garden. The bench where I was waiting for Sunny is my favourite place to sit. It's near a huge bougainvillaea. A bougainvillaea, in case you've never seen one, is a combination of a tree and a vine, and it's covered with gorgeous pink flowers. The one in the courtyard climbs up a trellis by the window of the school library. Hummingbirds love bougain-villaea, and a few were hovering around that day. Hummingbirds at school! I love California.

"Hey, girl!" said Sunny, dashing into the courtyard. "Ready to boogie?"

"You bet," I said. "We'd better run, too, if we're going to catch that bus."

To reach the beach, we had to meet the bus (really a mini-van) for the children's programme at a nearby primary school. It picks up several kids there, and then winds its way towards the beach, picking up kids at other schools on the way.

Sunny and I hurried to the school and climbed into the waiting van. Stephie, Erick and Ryan were already in the van, with a ten-year-old boy called Tyler and a six-year-old girl called Sara.

"Hi, Dawn!" called Erick, who was kneeling on his seat. "Want to see my new Turtle?" He held up a little figure.

"Nice," I said. "But I think it's time to sit down and fasten your seat-belt." The driver had climbed into the van. She closed the doors, and we were off to our next stop.

About forty-five minutes later—forty-five *long* minutes of hearing Erick and Ryan fight over the toys they had brought and listening to Stephie and a girl called Ruby (whom we had picked up at the next school) giggle endlessly—we arrived at the beach. Sunny and I slathered suntan lotion on the kids, made sure each one was holding the right beach bag, and then herded them over to the roped-off area where the children's programme meets.

The programme organizer, a woman called Alyssa, was already there, along with about twenty other kids. Alyssa's assistant, a guy called Dean, was teaching the kids how to play "Duck, Duck, Goose" in the sand, with another teen helper, Sondra. Erick, Ryan and the other kids from our van joined in straight away, and Sunny and I did whatever we could to help with the crowd of children.

First, while the game was going on, we put out juice and biscuits for a snack. Then I took one of the youngest girls to the toilet while Sunny and Alyssa seated everyone in a circle. They passed around the juice and biscuits, and tried to quieten everyone down a little. After the snack, I helped with another game—this time it was "Twenty Questions"—while the kids digested their food. About half an hour later, we took the kids to the changing room to change into their swimming suits, and then brought them down to the water. Most of them just paddled and splashed around, but a few of the older kids are good enough swimmers to venture out a little deeper. Alyssa had made sure each of the helpers knew exactly which kids they were responsible for, and we were careful to keep a close eye on them all.

Being at the beach with a lot of kids is fun. Kids love the sand and the sea, and they never seem to get bored or whiny. I ran and jumped with them, and threw a beach ball around. I helped them build a gigantic sand castle. I even let the kids bury me in the sand. Sunny took Stephie, Ruby and Tyler on a beachcombing walk, looking for shells and pebbles.

After an hour or so, Alyssa told Sunny and me that we were free to go. Many of the kids had been picked up by their parents, and the rest were having a quiet time under the shade of a big awning. The bus would be leaving in another hour, which left Sunny and me just enough time to hire boards and practise a bit.

We made our way to the surf shop. The beach was pretty crowded, and I saw a cluster of surfers near one end, where the waves were the best that day. "Looks like a good day for surfing," I said. "The waves are perfect. Not too big, but not too small, either."

Sunny grinned. "Perfect," she agreed.

We pushed open the shop door, and when the bell jingled the person at the counter looked up at us. It was that guy, Thrash. Sunny nudged me, but I ignored her. I didn't want Thrash to think I was some silly kid. I wanted him to think I was cool. Like he was. Seeing him up close, I could tell that Thrash was about twenty, and tall—maybe six feet two—with shoulder-length white-blond hair. He was incredibly tanned, and his blue eyes were intense in his brown face. He had three holes pierced in his right ear and two in his left—one more than me! (I've got two in each ear.) And he was wearing a wild-looking copper ring that looked like a snake twining around his middle finger. I suppose he was good-looking, but definitely not my type. Too wild, too old, and too—well, just too-too. Still, I found him fascinating. I wondered what his real name was. I mean, could his parents actually have called him Thrash?

Trying to look as if I knew what I was doing, I strolled over to the spot where the rentals boards are kept, and started to check them over. "I've been thinking about using a bigger board," I said to Sunny. "These 'guns' are cool, aren't they?"

"Guns" are what surfers call large, long boards.

"Those boards are only good for the really big screamers," said Thrash, stepping up behind me.

Screamers? I decided he must mean waves. "Oh," I said.

"You'll do best on a tri-fin, like this one." Thrash pointed to a neon pink board. "Really stable, even if you run into something gnarly out there."

Gnarly? I was going to have to study my surfer slang.

"Call me when you're ready," Thrash said. He went back into the repair part of the shop, where I'd seen him the other day. He started to rub wax on a board (surfers use it to keep from falling off their slippery boards), and I could tell it was *his* board by the loving way he applied the wax. The board was as distinctive as its owner. It was purple, with black designs that looked like primitive tribal tattoos. I hadn't seen anything like it. I walked a little closer to Thrash so I could see what he was doing. Taking care of a surfboard is a big part of surfing, but I didn't know much about it, as I'd been hiring my boards.

"Cool-looking wax," I said, pointing to the can he was dipping into. The can was black, with a picture of a skull and crossbones in white on the front. I'd never seen wax like that before, either.

"Custom-blended by this old guy down in Waimea," said Thrash. "I tell him what I want, and he makes it up for me. Costs a lot, but it helps me win contests, so I suppose it's worth it."

"Where's Waimea?" I asked.

"Hawaii," he said. "Monster waves down there. Much bigger than the ones at Kira Point."

"Where's—?" I began.

"Down Under. Australia," he replied, before I could ask. I realized that Thrash had probably surfed all around the world. He was one of those guys who travels everywhere in search of the perfect wave. And I had a feeling he'd won a lot of competitions.

I could have hung around listening to Thrash talk about surfing all afternoon, but I could see that Sunny was getting restless. We chose our boards, paid for them, and headed for the door.

"Take it easy, Kelea," said Thrash, grinning at me.

"Kelea?" I repeated.

"A legendary Hawaiian princess who made friends with the water god. She was a radical surfer," he said.

"Oh," I replied, blushing. "Well, thanks. I suppose I'd better practise if I want to live up to that name."

Sunny nudged me again as we walked to the water. "I think he likes you," she said.

"No way. He's a great guy, though, isn't he?"

"From what I hear, he's kind of tough. The guys say he's got into some fights since he's been here. He doesn't care about anything except surfing, and if you get in his way, watch out!" Sunny grimaced. "You'd better not get mixed up with him," she added.

"I won't," I said. "I just want to talk to him."

By that time, we'd reached the area where the surfers were hanging around. Some kids from my school were there, and plenty from the high school, including some kids Stacey had surfed with when she was visiting. They're rather wild. Stacey even got into a car accident when she was driving to the beach with them one day. Still, they're basically good kids. "Hi, Paul," I said to one of them. "Is Alana here today?"

"She's out there," he said, pointing to the waves. "With Rosemary. Carter and I are just about to paddle out. Want to come?"

"Okay," I said. My heart was beating fast at the very thought of riding through the waves. Suddenly, I couldn't wait to get into the water.

30

Stacey, you wouldn't believe the waves today,
I wrote when I got home. I wanted to send
off the letter the next morning, so I decided
to finish it.

Truly awesome. I wiped out
once, but I held my breath
and only got about three
gallons of water up my nose.
No problem! I'm improving,
I think. Not that I'll win
any prizes in the competition,
but at least I won't embar-
rass myself. Next time I
write I'll tell you about this
cool surfer dude I met. His
name's Thrash...

4th CHAPTER

Thursday

Dear Kristy,
   I wish you were here. Boy,
do I wish you were here.
Something terrible happened,
and somehow I think you
might be able to help me
understand it or figure it
out. You're always so practical,
and full of good ideas.
Anyway, what happened was
that this guy Thrash, a surfer,
had a terrible accident. He
might even be — oh, I can't
write the word. I just wish
I knew what to do.

It was Thursday afternoon when I heard the news. Sunny and I had arrived at the beach, all ready to have a great time with the kids in the programme. Alyssa had planned some terrific activities.

Sunny and I were just getting settled at the spot where the children's programme meets when Rosemary, one of the surfers from the high school, ran across the sand to us. She looked upset. "Can you believe it?" she said. "Nothing like this has ever happened on our beach. No way am I going into the water today. I mean, what if it was a shark?"

"Whoa!" said Sunny. "What are you talking about?"

"Haven't you heard?" asked Rosemary. "It's Thrash."

"Thrash?" I repeated, feeling scared all of a sudden. "What? What's happened to him?"

"He's dead," said Rosemary.

"*What?*" cried Sunny and I together. And I added, "Dead? You're crazy. Thrash can't be dead. I just saw him yesterday."

"It happened last night," said Rosemary. "Well, I *suppose* it was last night."

"*What* happened?" asked Sunny. Both of us were just standing there with our mouths wide open. Kids from the programme were running around nearby, kicking up sand that stung my ankles, but I ignored them.

"Nobody's sure, exactly," said Rosemary. "His board was washed up on the beach today, and it's all mangled. And Thrash has disappeared."

"What was that you said about sharks?" I asked.

"That's what some people think might have happened to him," said Rosemary. "The way his board was all chopped up, it looked as if he could have been attacked by a shark."

I was stunned. "No way! I'm sure he's around somewhere."

"The police have been searching all day," said Rosemary. "There's no sign of him anywhere."

"But a *shark*?" asked Sunny. "There aren't any sharks here, are there?"

Rosemary shrugged. "Who knows? Anyway, maybe it wasn't a shark. Maybe he just fell off his board. Maybe his board hit him on the head and he drowned in the undertow. It's pretty wicked sometimes, especially down by the breakwater, where he likes to surf. I mean—*liked* to surf." She shrugged again. "Anyway, he won't be surfing any more."

I couldn't believe it was true. Thrash was the best surfer around. How could he fall?

"Gotta run!" said Rosemary. "Sorry for the bad news." She turned to leave.

"Wait a minute," I said. "Isn't there something we can do? I mean, to help find Thrash?"

"What can *we* do?" she replied. "The police are on the case. This is their job."

Rosemary left, and Sunny and I exchanged glances. This was upsetting news. We looked around to make sure none of the kids had heard it, and luckily they all seemed to be involved in building a long, twisting sand dragon. Dean was supervising, while Alyssa sat under an umbrella reading to a few kids who didn't feel like playing in the sand. "I'm glad none of them heard about *that*," I said to Sunny.

Just then I felt a little hand slip into mine. There was Stephie, looking up at me. "Dawn?" she said. "What's happened? Has something bad happened?"

"Oh, Stephie," I said. She was the last kid I would have wanted to hear the news. Sometimes emotional stress can bring on one of Stephie's asthma attacks. I thought fast. "Everything's okay," I said. "One of the surfers might have had a little accident, but I'm sure he'll be fine."

"Is that why everybody's over there?" Stephie pointed down the beach, to a spot where a large crowd had gathered. I saw two or three policemen, and they looked awfully strange on the beach, wearing their dark blue uniforms, surrounded by people dressed in swimsuits.

"Yes," I said. "Do you think the policemen are going to go surfing dressed like that?"

Stephie giggled. "They'd look pretty funny if they did." She looked at the crowd and giggled again. "Do you think they'd even wear their hats?" she said. Then she ran off to join the dragon-builders.

"Phew!" I said to Sunny. "That was close. We'd better try not to let the kids get wind of this. Oh, and we probably shouldn't take them swimming today, just in case. But I'm almost sure there aren't any sharks. Aren't you?"

She nodded. "But it might be good to wait a day and see what the beach patrol says. I'll tell Alyssa. She's finished reading that story—perhaps I can get her alone for a minute."

Sunny ran off to talk to Alyssa, but I just stood and watched the crowd, which continued to grow. Several more police officers were there now. A couple of them were talking to the surfers who had gathered, and three others were walking down the beach—probably looking for clues. Then I saw two officers dragging something up off the beach, towards a police van. I squinted to get a better look. "Oh!" I said out loud, when I'd worked out what they were dragging. It was Thrash's surfboard. There was no mistaking it. And it was dreadfully mangled. The fins looked broken and the nose (that's the front part) had a huge dent. Suddenly I felt sick.

What if Thrash were really dead? How awful. I studied the waves crashing on the shore. They didn't *look* lethal. They were smooth and regular, and people surfed on them every day. All right, so I'd heard about small accidents happening once in a while, but I'd never heard of anyone being badly hurt, let alone . . . For a minute, I thought about giving up my surfing lessons. After all, if *Thrash* could get killed riding the waves, anyone could. But then I got a grip on myself. I was just a beginner, I reminded myself, and I never tried anything fancy. I only went in the water when the surf was mild and regular, the way it was that day. And there were always lots of people around, looking out for each other. I knew I'd be okay.

"Dawn!" I heard Sunny call. I jumped. I'd been thinking so hard that I'd almost forgotten about my responsibilities with the kids.

"Coming!" I said. I took one last look at the waves, and one more down the beach, towards the crowd. Then I joined Sunny.

"I've spoken to Alyssa," she said. "She agrees with us, so we're going to keep the kids out of the water. We'll hold relay races and play Mother May I instead of swimming. Want to help me set up a course for the races?"

"Okay," I replied. Sunny and I worked for a few minutes, but I couldn't concentrate. I kept thinking about what had happened to Thrash, and I decided I had to find out more. "Sunny," I said. "I want to go down there and find out what the police are saying. Is that okay with you, if Alyssa says I can go? I'll be back in fifteen minutes."

"Of course," said Sunny, giving me a curious look. "Hey, you—you didn't have a crush on him or anything, did you?"

"Definitely not," I said. "I only talked to him once! I just thought he was an interesting person." I couldn't believe I was saying "was" instead of "is".

I walked over to Alyssa and asked if I could be excused from my duties for a few minutes. I promised to stay and work a little late that day, instead of running off to surf. She agreed, and I made my way down the beach.

As I drew closer to the crowd, I could see that the police were still talking to the surfers. Surfers who weren't being questioned were standing around in twos and threes, talking among themselves. I walked past one of those groups, hoping to hear what they were saying. Most of the good surfers were like minor celebrities on the beach, so I knew their names.

"Man, that dude was radical," said TJ, a guy with spiked brown hair and a dangling earring.

"Totally," agreed Wanda, who's one of the best surfers—male *or* female.

"He *used* to be," said this guy called Gonzo, who was wearing wildly patterned shorts. "But he was over the hill. I mean, I can bust moves he never even thought of. I was going to beat him in that competition, and he knew it. I bet you anything he just left town so he wouldn't have to face the humiliation."

This other guy called Spanky, who wears a nose-ring, nodded in agreement.

I raised my eyebrows. *That* was an interesting theory. In a way, I hoped it was true, because it would mean Thrash wasn't dead. But I hated to think he might not be the best surfer around. I decided Gonzo was probably just jealous.

I tried to listen to the police for a while without looking too conspicuous, but I didn't pick up much information. To tell the truth, they didn't seem very worried about Thrash. I overheard one officer refer to him as "that bum", and another speculate that he'd probably just moved on to the next beach.

I thought that was pretty interesting, too, and I wanted to poke around some more, but I knew my time was up, so I jogged back to the kids and joined Sunny as she supervised the relay races.

That afternoon I couldn't get Thrash out of my mind. When I got back home, I ran straight for the newspaper to see if I could find any news about the accident. There was an article on the front page! I read it eagerly, wondering what clues had been found to the mystery. And then my eye fell on one paragraph that was so interesting I read it three times. It quoted a police detective, who discussed the possibility that Thrash's board had been tampered with. He didn't say *who* might have done it, or even if he was sure it had happened, but he did say it was a possibility. From that moment on, I knew I had to find out the truth, whatever it took. I needed to know whether Thrash's death had been an accident—or if he'd been murdered.

5th CHAPTER

Saturday

Dear Dawn,
I'm going to have to call
you some night soon,
that is, if my dad will
let me run up the
phone bill a little more.
Why? Because I have
a long story to tell you,
about sitting for Marilyn
and Carolyn Arnold. I
already wrote it up for
the club notebook, and it
would take me a long
time to write it up again.

I'll just say that there was an accident — not a terrible one, but an accident. And it wasn't really anybody's fault — it just happened. But I think it may affect the twins' relationship. How? I'm not sure yet, but I have a feeling it will.

Talk to you soon!

Love and xxx ooo,
Mary Anne

I heard from Mary Anne the day after I got her letter. She told me the whole story. Marilyn and Carolyn Arnold are eight-year-old identical twins. The BSC sits for them quite often. When we first started sitting for them, Mrs Arnold insisted on dressing them alike and treating them almost as one person. They had the same hairstyle, and they shared a room which was split down the middle into identical halves. Since then, they've worked hard to establish separate personalities. Each girl always had her own interests—Marilyn plays the piano, for example, and Carolyn likes science— but now they're even more distinct. Marilyn grew her hair long, and she likes wearing simple, comfortable clothes. Her room (each twin has her own room now) is yellow. And Carolyn got a cool new haircut and some trendy clothes, and *her* room's blue, with a cat motif.

Anyway, as I was saying, when I spoke to Mary Anne I heard what had happened to the twins that Saturday morning. Mary Anne had a sitting job at the Arnolds', starting at ten that morning. She arrived at a quarter to (we're always punctual, as it's good for business, and we even try to be early when we can), and Mrs Arnold greeted her at the door. "Oh, I'm so glad you're early," she said. "Now *I* can get going early, too. My meeting should be over about four, so I'll be home soon after that." She bustled around, getting ready to leave. "The girls are in the basement, and I know they can't wait to show you what they're doing down there."

Just then, Carolyn came pounding up the stairs. "Mary Anne!" she cried. "Wait till you see our gymnastics stuff!"

Mary Anne smiled. "Gymnastics stuff?"

"Me and Marilyn are going to gym classes, and we love it," Carolyn explained. "So Mum and Dad got us all this great equipment!"

Mrs Arnold smiled at Mary Anne. "We're so glad they've got an interest in common," she said. "Just remember," she added, turning to Carolyn, "the rules about playing down there, okay?"

Carolyn made a face. "Of course," she said. "And we're not *playing*. We're working on our routines."

"Right," said Mrs Arnold. "How could I have forgotten?" She grinned at Mary Anne over Carolyn's head. "I'd better run," she said, bending to kiss Carolyn. "Be good."

"I will," Carolyn answered impatiently. "Come *on*, Mary Anne." She grabbed Mary Anne's hand and dragged her towards the basement door.

Mary Anne let herself be pulled. She was curious about what kind of equipment the Arnolds had bought. Was their basement really big enough for a vaulting horse and parallel bars?

"See?" Carolyn asked, when she and Mary Anne reached the bottom of the stairs.

"Isn't this cool?" said Marilyn, running up to them. "We've got mats, and a balancing beam, and everything!"

"I see," said Mary Anne. She looked around, impressed. The Arnolds had made the basement into a mini-gymnastics centre. As well as the mats and the balancing beam (which was a low one, only about fifteen centimetres off the floor), there was a big mirror leaning against one wall, and a cassette player, obviously secondhand, on a table. "You're all set up here, aren't you?"

Marilyn and Carolyn grinned. Then Marilyn ran to the balancing beam. "Look what I can do!" she cried, ready to step up on it.

"No, watch me!" said Carolyn, heading for the mats as if she were about to start somersaulting backwards.

"Hang on," said Mary Anne. "I can't watch both of you at the same time. You'll have to take turns. Also, didn't I hear your mum mention something about rules?" She folded her arms and waited.

"Oh, right," said Marilyn.

"The rules are easy," said Carolyn. "Just like in our real gym."

"Tell me about them," said Mary Anne.

"Well, only one person is supposed to go at a time," said Marilyn, blushing a little.

"And the other person's supposed to spot the person who's tumbling or walking along the beam," added Carolyn, who was wearing an identical blush.

Mary Anne nodded. "What does 'spotting' mean, exactly?" she asked, even though she was pretty sure she knew.

"Well, if Carolyn's doing a somersault, for example, I stand near her so I can help her over if she has any trouble," said Marilyn.

"Or, if Marilyn's on the balancing beam, I walk beside her so she can use me for help if she needs it," said Carolyn. "Even professionals use spotters," she added. "It's the first thing we learned about."

"Well, good," said Mary Anne. "Now you just need to remember to do it, every time. Right?"

"Right," chorused the twins.

"Okay," said Mary Anne. "Let's see what you can do. Who wants to go first?"

"Me!" said both girls. Then they looked at each other and giggled. "You can go," said Marilyn. "I need a little rest, anyway."

The twins are like that, sometimes. They get along well, and they know how to share things. I think that must come from growing up with another person *right there* all the time. If you didn't learn to share, you'd go crazy because you'd be fighting every minute.

Carolyn poised herself on the mat while Marilyn stood nearby, watching carefully. Then she turned a whole series of back somersaults and, Mary Anne told me later, she did them very well. When she'd finished, she stood up with a proud look on her face, pulling herself into the pose that gymnasts go into when they've finished a routine: arms up, chest out, feet together. Mary Anne clapped loudly.

"Now me," said Marilyn. She walked to the balancing beam, mounted it and began to step along it carefully with her arms out for balance. Carolyn walked next to her, and once Mary Anne saw Marilyn reach down and steady herself by touching Carolyn's shoulder. After a fairly impressive front "walkover" (she started in a back bend and then pushed up and over), Marilyn finished her "routine", jumped off the beam, and flung herself into the "finish" pose.

Mary Anne applauded. "Great job, girls!" she said.

"That's not even our real routine, either," said Carolyn. "We've got this whole thing we worked out, with music." She ran to the cassette player and pressed a button. An old rock song, "Tutti Frutti", came on, and Carolyn ran back to the mats to show Mary Anne the "real" routine. She mounted the balancing beam, and Marilyn stood beside her.

Just then, Mary Anne heard the phone ring. "You two be careful," she said. "I'll be right back." She ran up the stairs to answer the phone. While she was taking a message for Mr Arnold, she noticed that the music in the basement stopped and started a couple of times. And then, as she was ringing off, she heard a sharp, short yell from downstairs. "Uh-oh!" she said. She raced back to the basement and found Carolyn lying on the floor, crying.

Marilyn was crying, too. "It's my fault,"

she howled. "I was supposed to be spotting her, but the cassette player wasn't working properly so I tried to mend it."

"I was doing a walkover, and then I fell!" wailed Carolyn. She wriggled her foot. "Oh, my ankle. It *hurts*!"

Mary Anne bent to look at the ankle. It was already swelling. "Oh, no," she said. "Can you stand on it?" She tried to help Carolyn up, but Carolyn collapsed in a heap.

"I bet it's broken," said Marilyn, still crying.

Mary Anne thought Marilyn might be right, but she didn't say so. Instead, she and Marilyn helped Carolyn up the stairs and into a chair, propping her ankle up on another chair. Mary Anne got some ice out of the freezer, wrapped it in a plastic bag, and told Carolyn to hold it on her ankle. Then she rang home. "Sharon," she said to my mum. "I need help."

"I'm on my way," my mum replied, when Mary Anne finished explaining what had happened.

Next Mary Anne rang Mrs Arnold at her meeting and told her they were on their way to casualty. By the time my mum, Mary Anne, Marilyn and Carolyn reached the hospital, Mrs *and* Mr Arnold were there, too.

Carolyn's ankle wasn't broken, luckily.

But it was badly sprained, and she was sent home with crutches and told to stay off it for a while. As they were all leaving the hospital, Mary Anne heard Marilyn say something that took her by surprise. She told me on the phone that night that she thought the twins' relationship was going to be closer than ever from now on. Maybe *too* close.

"I'm *sorry*," Marilyn had said, sniffing. She was talking to Carolyn. "It's all my fault, and I swear I will never, ever, *ever* leave your side again."

6th CHAPTER

Saturday

Dear Claudia,
   I wish you were here to
help me figure out what
to wear to this party I'm
going to tonight. It's a
beach party, so it's not
exactly formal, but I do
want to look nice. And I
have to think about layers,
since it gets cool on the
beach as the sun goes
down. I know you'd come
up with something fantastic,
but I guess since you're not
here to help me I'll just
wear my usual outfit:

*shorts and a T-shirt, with
sweatpants and a big white
sweater for later. Maybe
I'll add those cool seashell
earrings you made for me!*
                    Love, Dawn

Sunny and I were excited about the beach
party. It was sponsored by the beach club,
the one that runs the children's programme.
All the kids would be having a cookout on
the beach while their parents went to a luau
in the club dining room. (A luau, in case you
don't know, is like a barbecue, Hawaiian
style.) Alyssa, Dean, Sondra, Sunny and I
had put a lot of planning into the kids'
cookout, as we wanted to make it extra
special for them. Sunny had phoned me at
least three times that Saturday, to make sure
we had everything we needed. We were
bringing hot dogs and hamburgers, tofu
dogs and veggie burgers. We were going to
toast marshmallows over the camp fire. And
we were brushing up on our favourite ghost
stories, so we could tell them after darkness
fell.

That evening, Sunny and her mum
picked me up at Dad's house. With Alyssa's
permission, I'd invited Jeff to our cookout,
but he'd decided not to come. He was
planning to go out with his skateboarding
friends, instead.

"See you!" I called to my dad and Jeff, as I gathered my things together and ran to the car. I jumped into the back seat, and Sunny turned to grin at me.

"It's a perfect night for a beach party," she said. "This is going to be great."

"You girls aren't going to go into the water, are you?" asked Sunny's mum, looking rather worried.

"No way," I said. "It's too cold at night for swimming."

"I'm going to stay near that camp fire," said Sunny.

By the time we arrived at the beach, most of the kids were already there, gathered around the fire pit that Alyssa and Dean had dug. The older kids had been put to work gathering driftwood, and the younger ones were playing tag around the growing pile that would soon be a bonfire.

"Dawn! Sunny!" said Alyssa. "Just in time. Sondra was just going to take some of the kids on a beach clean-up walk, and Dean's going to show another group how to make seashell chimes. Why don't each of you join a group, and help?"

Sunny set off with Sondra, Ruby, Stephie and about six other kids. They were armed with rakes and shovels and bags for collecting rubbish. "It's important to keep the beach clean," I heard Sondra saying as they walked off. "It's everybody's responsibility. See this?" She picked up a set of plastic rings that had once held together a six-pack of lemonade. "A fish or a turtle could get tangled up in this and die." She put it into her bag, and led the kids down the beach. I watched them go, and saw them stooping every few paces to pick things up and put them into their bags.

Dean and I led the other group of kids, which included Sara, Erick and Ryan, in the opposite direction, to look for shells. As we were going to make wind chimes, Dean told us to look for shells with holes in them. He was carrying a large bucket for collecting, and as the kids dropped shells in it he told us what kind they were and what type of animal had lived in them. Dean seemed to know a lot about marine life. When I asked him why, he told me he planned to be a marine biologist one day. "I want to make sure all these species survive," he said, holding a delicate shell in his hand so I could see the colours in it.

Erick and Ryan were behaving pretty well, for once. "Look what I've found!" said Erick, running to me with a shell.

"Beautiful," I said. It *was* beautiful. It was white, with a creamy pink interior.

"It's for you," said Erick shyly. Then he ran off.

"I think somebody's got a crush on you," Dean said, with a grin.

I blushed and bent my head to look for more shells. Soon we'd gathered a big bucketful, and we turned back. Dean had set up a work area near the bonfire site. There were pieces of driftwood to hang the shells from, and fishing line to tie them with. We started the kids on their chimes, and soon we were busy helping to thread line through holes in the shells, tying knots, and advising kids on how to arrange the shells so that the wind would bump them together.

After a while, Sunny and Sondra came back with their group. The kids were proud of all the rubbish they'd collected. Each one was lugging a full bag, and Sunny and Sondra were carrying extras. "*That* part of the beach is a lot cleaner," said Sunny with satisfaction.

"But we would have to do that every single day, over the whole beach, to keep it really clean," said Stephie, a little dejectedly. "Now I understand why it's bad to leave even just one little paper cup on the beach. What a mess!"

Sunny and Sondra and I started talking about making posters that would let other beachgoers know why it was important not to leave litter. The kids thought that would be a great project, and before long we'd planned a programme of beach activities for the following week.

Alyssa joined us after a while. "It's getting near dinnertime," she said. "Sunny and Dawn, would you two spread out those blankets so we can sit on them while we eat? Dean and Sondra and I will start the fire and get the food ready for the barbecue."

"Okay," I replied. Sunny and I set to work. Enticing smells were already drifting out of the beach club dining room, where the luau was under way. I was hungry, and the thought of a veggie burger hot off the fire kept me working fast. By the time Sunny and I had finished our job, the fire was ready to be lit.

"Stand back, everybody," said Dean. He bent to light the fire, and the dry wood caught immediately.

"Ohh!" said the kids, as they watched the flames rising into the darkening sky.

"Pretty!" said Stephie. "And warm." She held her hands out towards the fire. The sun was going down, and I noticed that there was a chill in the air. A thin white mist was beginning to rise over the sea. Sunny and I got busy matching kids up with their sweaters and jackets and helping the younger ones with their buttons and zips.

Erick and Ryan and some of the other kids began a wild dance around the bonfire, yelling and throwing their hands in the air. Alyssa shook her head, smiling. "Might as well let them go ahead," she said. "They'll burn off some energy." The younger kids chose a blanket near the fire and sat quietly, watching the flames.

It wasn't long before the fire had burnt down enough to cook on. Sunny and I skewered hot dogs on sticks and held them over the coals, while Dean set up a grill for burgers. As each round was finished, we handed the food out to the kids, who wolfed it down as fast as we could cook it. At last they were all fed. Then we ate our own dinner, and I must say that I've never had a veggie burger that tasted quite so good. The combination of a busy evening, the salt air coming off the sea, and the warm, glowing bonfire seemed to make me incredibly hungry.

The kids settled into a quieter mood as we began toasting marshmallows. Some of the younger ones even dozed off. I saw Ruby sleeping with her head on Stephie's lap. Sunny and I walked around the circle of kids, making sure everyone was warm and cosy. I put on my tracksuit trousers and pulled a big sweater over my head. The moon was rising by then, and the beach had become eerie-looking and chilly.

"Time for ghost stories," said Alyssa, her face alight in the glow of the fire. "Anybody know a good one?"

"I do! I do!" said Erick. "Can I go first?"

Alyssa nodded, and Erick began that old story about the spook who's walking up the stairs, step by step, slowly, slowly—until he *gets you*! The kids shrieked and giggled at the surprise ending. Then another boy called Justin began to tell a story about a swamp monster that glowed in the dark.

I smiled at Sunny. I was pretty sure she was thinking what I was thinking—this was the perfect setting for ghost stories. Of course, the stories that the kids were telling were fairly tame, not like some I know. I think I've read every ghost story in the world, and I prefer the really scary ones. But no ghost story is as good as a real ghost. I thought about the ghost that might haunt my old farmhouse back in Stoneybrook. There's a secret passage in that house—did I mention it?—and some people think the ghost of the crazy son of one of the previous owners may haunt it. His name's Jared Mulray, and he's supposed to have died of a broken heart. I'm pretty sure I've heard him once or twice, but I haven't had an actual sighting yet. If I do, it will be one of the best moments of my life—even if it scares the pants off me.

My thoughts were interrupted by a cry from Erick. "Look at that!" he said, pointing out to sea. I turned to look, and caught a glimpse of a faraway movement, though it was hard to make out much through the mist.

Within seconds, everybody was on their feet. (Everybody except the little kids who were asleep, of course.) We stared out at the breakers, trying to work out what we were seeing.

"It's a surfer," Sunny said under her breath.

"But why would anybody be surfing on this kind of night?" wondered Alyssa.

Alyssa was right. It was hardly an ideal night for surfing, with all that mist. And even with the moon shining, it was pretty dark.

I looked again, but I couldn't see anything this time. Erick began to run, leading a group of kids along the beach towards the spot where we'd last seen the figure. Sunny and I followed them. By the time we arrived at the water's edge, nothing was to be seen out on the ocean.

"A ghost!" said Erick. "It was a ghost, I bet you anything."

"A surfer ghost?" said Sunny.

"I bet it's the ghost of Thrash," I said quietly. I was hugging myself, trying not to stay warm. Suddenly, I couldn't stop shivering.

We herded the kids back to the bonfire, trying to calm them down so that they wouldn't scare any younger kids who had woken up.

Soon after that, the beach party ended. Alyssa gave Sunny and me a ride home, and on the way we discussed the "surfer ghost". Even though Sunny loves ghost stories, she doesn't believe in *real* ghosts. She and Alyssa were positive there was a perfectly good explanation for whatever we'd seen. For example, Alyssa thought it might have been a dolphin.

But I wasn't so sure.

Over the next week, the kids at the beach programme were full of speculation about the surfer ghost. The story grew, and soon other people were reporting sightings. Even at school, it was all anybody talked about. I think a lot of people were just having fun with the story, but I took it seriously. I *knew* I'd seen something that night. It *looked* like a ghost. And if it was a surfing ghost, it could have been the ghost of Thrash. His spirit might be haunting our beach. This could be the best ghost story yet!

7th CHAPTER

Friday

Dear Jessi,
   Boy, have I got a mystery on my hands! And maybe a really good ghost story, too. I wish you and everyone in the BSC could be here to help me figure this one out. How's good old Stoneybrook? I miss it — and you, too.

Love, Dawn

I was trying to write regularly to all my friends back home, even though telling them everything that was going on was becoming harder. Too much was happening to be able to write it in one letter. What I really needed was to sit down with my friends and go over the facts, which is what I would do if I were back in Stoneybrook. The BSC's got a great record for solving mysteries. But this time, I was on my own. Oh, I had Sunny and the We ♥ Kids Club, but it just wasn't the same. First of all, Sunny refused point blank to believe in ghosts. And she and Maggie and Jill don't seem to get as excited about mysteries as my Connecticut friends do.

No, if I were going to find out what had happened to Thrash, I would have to do it by myself. I'd thought about it a lot since the day I heard he'd vanished. The sighting of the ghost surfer, and the talk about it afterwards, only added to my curiosity. Here's what I was thinking: first of all, Thrash had disappeared without trace. Secondly, I'd seen his mangled surfboard. Thirdly, I'd read in the paper that the police believed the board might have been tampered with. And fourthly, a ghostly surfer was now riding the very waves that Thrash had last ridden.

Conclusion? Don't think I'm silly, but I'd started to believe that Thrash had been murdered and his spirit was going to haunt the beach until the murderer was caught. That's a pretty common theme in ghost stories. Somebody gets stabbed, or poisoned, or whatever. The murderer thinks he's committed the perfect crime, and will never be found out. He goes on his merry way. But *then*, things begin to happen. He starts seeing images behind him in the mirror, or a hand appearing out of nowhere. Or he hears footsteps, and eerie wails. Books start to fall off his bookshelves, all by themselves, and doors open even when nobody's around. Eventually, of course, the murderer's driven completely crazy by all this, and he runs to the nearest police station and confesses everything. He's arrested, and the ghost of the murdered person is finally at rest.

I decided that whoever murdered Thrash might be feeling tortured by the fact that a surfer ghost was riding the waves at the beach. But obviously, he (or *she*) wasn't feeling tortured *enough*, because he hadn't confessed yet. That left it to me to discover who the guilty party was, and to help matters along. After all, being a spirit wandering around waiting to be put to rest can't be much fun. Thrash might have been a surfer bum, but he deserved a better fate than that.

For more than a week after the beach

party, I thought about the mystery every day. I thought about it as I brushed my teeth in the morning, and as I sat in my classroom at school. I thought about it through my classes—and almost failed a maths test! I thought about it while I was working at the beach programme, but I made sure to watch closely over the kids I was responsible for at the same time. And at night, I dreamed about it. I dreamed about a surfer ghost, knifing through ghostly waves on a ghostly surfboard. One morning I woke up giggling because I'd been wondering, in my dream, whether the ghost wore glow-in-the-dark shorts when he surfed.

But all that thinking wasn't getting me anywhere. It was time to take action. I decided that I should talk to the police and make sure I wasn't missing any important information.

One afternoon, towards the end of our shift at the beach programme, I told Sunny I was going to miss our surfing lesson that day.

"Why?" she asked. "You're getting really good, and Buck says it's important to keep practising now, with the competition coming up soon."

"I know," I replied, "but I've got to do something really important. I want to talk to the police about Thrash."

"Oh, Thrash," said Sunny, giving me an exasperated glance. She'd decided I'd been madly in love with Thrash, and that I wasn't "over" his death. "You've got to let him go," she said. "Get on with your life."

I'd given up trying to tell Sunny that Thrash hadn't been my type. I'd also given up trying to persuade her to help me solve the mystery. She just didn't seem all that interested. "I really need to do this," I said firmly. "It's important to me."

Sunny shrugged. "Okay. Shall I tell Buck you'll be there tomorrow?"

"Of course," I said, even though I wasn't positive I would be. That would depend on what I found out from the police.

When I'd finished at the beach programme, I walked to the police station, which is a few streets away from the beach. The station looked quite different from the one in Stoneybrook. For one thing, among the ordinary patrol cars parked outside were several dune buggies painted in police colours. Around here, the police have to patrol the beach as well as the streets. And when I went inside, I noticed that the atmosphere was a little more informal than in Connecticut. The officers wore short-sleeved uniforms. They seemed pretty friendly, too.

"What can I do for you?" asked the officer at the front desk.

"I'm interested in the case of the surfer who disappeared," I said. I'd already decided that I wouldn't say anything to the police about a surfing ghost. I didn't want them to think I was a nutcase.

"Surfer, surfer," muttered the officer. "Can you be more specific?"

"You know," I said. "That guy whose board was washed up on the beach. Thrash."

"Oh," said the officer, leaning back in his chair and folding his hands behind his head. "You mean that drifter." He grinned. "What about him?"

I frowned. The officer didn't seem to be taking the case very seriously. "I just wanted to know if there were any new leads?"

"Leads?" he repeated. He shook his head. "Usually these things just blow over. I don't think anybody's even filed a missing-person's report on the guy."

"But—but—he's gone!" I said. "And his surfboard might have been tampered with. I wanted to find out what might have happened, like if there were high tides that night, or if there's some way to find out how the damage was done to his board."

By this time, another policeman had joined the first. He listened for a while, shaking his head. The one at the desk was hardly paying any attention. He was filling in some kind of paperwork now, checking a file on his desk for information. I glanced down at the notebook I was carrying. I didn't think I'd be getting any information to write in it. And then I heard the second policeman mutter something to the first.

"If he washes up, he washes up," was what I thought I heard him say. I looked at him, surprised, just in time to catch the two men grinning at each other.

Obviously, the police didn't care what had happened to Thrash. I was angry, but I knew there was no point in yelling at them. Instead, I just said, "Thank you" as frostily as I could, and left.

I didn't go to any surfing lessons for the rest of that week. I spent all my free time at the beach investigating the case on my own. I talked to the surf-fishermen and learned about the tides. I talked to Gonzo and the other surfers about how the waves broke on the shore. And I talked to the beach "regulars", the brown-skinned older men and women who spend all day, every day, on the beach.

Soon I'd worked out that *if* Thrash's body had washed up on the beach, it would have been down near the old pier, where big wooden pilings were still sticking out of the shallow water. I searched the area, hoping to find some sign of Thrash. I knew I would have heard if his body *had* been washed up, and I certainly wasn't expecting that it would now. But maybe I'd find *something*.

One day, when she didn't have a lesson, Sunny came with me on my tour of the beach. I told her what I was looking for.

"I don't know what you're trying to prove," she said.

"I'm not sure myself," I answered honestly. "I suppose I'm trying to prove that Thrash really is dead, and that he was murdered. And I'd like to work out who did it."

Sunny shook her head. "Just like Nancy Drew!" she said. "Aren't you afraid of getting mixed up with murderers?"

"I'll go to the police when the time's right," I said. "If and when I have any evidence. Meanwhile, nobody's going to worry about some teenage girl who looks like she's beachcombing."

"That's true," said Sunny.

We walked along quietly for a while, without finding anything. We'd made our way down to the old pier, and now we were working our way back to the spot where the surfers usually head into the water.

"Hey, look at this!" Sunny cried

suddenly. She bent down to pick up something. "I almost stubbed my toe on it. Why do people dump all their junk on the beach? I don't think those posters we made have helped at all."

I took the object from her hand and examined it. I'd known what it was from my first glance, but I wanted to be sure. "Do you know what this is?" I asked, holding up the small black-and-white can. "It's Thrash's wax. His personal, custom-made wax. Nobody else uses this."

Sunny looked at me wide-eyed. "What are you trying to say?" she asked.

"I don't know," I said. "Maybe the ghost is using it."

"Oooh!" said Sunny. "Scary! But unlikely. Maybe Thrash isn't really dead, and *he's* using it."

"Not dead?" I said.

"Yeah, maybe he faked his own death, like Gonzo said. Or maybe he got hurt, and he's got amnesia from bumping his head."

"Right." I grinned. "I think you may be watching too much TV. Anyway, this doesn't prove anything. It's a bit dented and rusty. It could have been lying there in the sand since before Thrash disappeared."

"That's probably it," said Sunny. "So, have we finished being detectives for the day? I'm hot, and I could do with a swim."

We tore off our T-shirts and ran into the cool water. I tried to let the waves wash my brain clear of all the confusing clues—or *non*-clues—I'd found, but I knew that I couldn't forget about the mystery. I had to keep investigating. I had to find out what had happened to Thrash.

8th CHAPTER

Tuesday

Dear Dawn,
    How are you?
We miss you so
much. I hope your
lessons are going
well. I just got
back from a sitting
job at the Arnolds',
and I'm about to
write it up for
the club notebook,
but I have a
feeling you'd get
a kick out of
hearing what's going
on with them. I

*guess you know
what happened when
Mary Anne sat
for them awhile
back. Well, you'll
never believe
what's happening
now ...*

Jessi wrote me a long, funny letter about her experiences at the Arnold house that day. She knew, of course, about Carolyn's accident and what Marilyn had said about "never leaving" her twin's side. She'd read the entry in the club notebook. But she was still unprepared for what she saw that afternoon.

She arrived on time at the Arnolds' and rang the bell. From inside, she heard Mrs Arnold call, "Marilyn, would you let Jessi in? I'm busy getting ready to go."

Jessi waited for what seemed like a long time. She was beginning to wonder if Marilyn had heard her mother. Perhaps she was in the basement, practising her gymnastics routine. But then, she heard noises in the hall—an uneven thumping sound, and a voice saying, "That's right, just take it easy. Good! Good!" And then Marilyn opened the door.

"Hi, Jessi," she said. Carolyn was standing beside her, leaning on her crutches and panting a little. "Hi!" she said, when she'd got her breath back.

"Hi, you two," Jessi replied. "Thanks for letting me in. But you didn't *both* have to come to the door."

"Yes, we did," said Marilyn. "Wherever I go, she goes. And wherever she goes, I go. We stick together. Anyway, the doctor said it was good for her to exercise a bit and not just sit around all the time."

Carolyn nodded. She looked tired, but she was smiling.

"How's your ankle?" asked Jessi.

"It's much better," Marilyn answered for her sister. "The doctor says it's healing very well."

Jessi grinned. "Thanks for the report, Nurse Marilyn. But I asked Carolyn. So, *Carolyn*, how is it?"

"Not too bad," said Carolyn. "At first it kept me awake at night, but it doesn't hurt so much any more."

"That's good," said Jessi. "You'll be off those crutches in no time."

"She's getting really good at them," said Marilyn. "And I can use them, too. Want to see?" Carolyn handed her a crutch, and the two of them hopped up and down the hall on one crutch each, giggling and shrieking as they went.

"Girls, girls," said Mrs Arnold, running down the stairs. "How about some quiet time now? I think Carolyn could do with a rest."

"That's right," said Marilyn, in her "nurse" voice. "You need a rest, now. Come on into the living room, and I'll get you settled." She gave the crutch back to Carolyn and led her along the hall, walking very slowly so that Carolyn could keep up.

"Well," said Jessi to Mrs Arnold, "Marilyn seems to be taking good care of her sister."

Mrs Arnold rolled her eyes. "You don't know the half of it," she said. "But you'll see how things are. I must fly. Would you make sure the girls get their homework done? Also, Marilyn needs to practise the piano, and Carolyn's got a science project to work on. They can have a snack first, though."

With that, Mrs Arnold left, and Jessi was alone with the girls. She made her way into the living room to check on them, and found Carolyn lying on the sofa propped up by five big cushions. Marilyn was fluffing up the sixth, getting ready to arrange it under Carolyn's head.

"Wow! You look pretty comfortable," said Jessi.

"She is," said Marilyn.

"I am," agreed Carolyn, smiling. She seemed to appreciate the attention her twin was giving her.

"Are you two ready for a snack?" asked Jessi.

"Of course!" said Marilyn. "I'll help you get it. Or—no, I'd better stay here with Carolyn."

"It's okay," said Carolyn.

Marilyn looked torn, so Jessi spoke up. "Why don't I prepare your snacks," she said. "I'll let you know when they're ready." She went into the kitchen and put some biscuits on a plate. Then she poured two glasses of milk and got out two bananas. "Ready!" she called to the girls.

Marilyn came running. "I'll bring Carolyn's to her," she said. She kept looking over her shoulder, back towards the living room, as if she were worried that Carolyn might disappear while she was away. In a flash she put the biscuits and milk and fruit on a tray. She added a vase with a red silk rose and stood back to see how it looked. "Perfect!" she said, picking it up.

Jessi raised her eyebrows. Then she followed Marilyn back to the living room and watched as Carolyn accepted the tray. Carolyn seemed to be getting used to her princess treatment.

"Would you like me to turn on the TV?" asked Marilyn. "You can choose whatever channel you want," she added generously.

"Let's not turn on the TV," said Jessi. "You two have got things to do. Why don't I help Carolyn with her homework upstairs, and Marilyn, you can start on your practising."

"*I'll* help her," insisted Marilyn. "I'm the only one who knows how."

Jessi didn't want to start an argument, so she let Marilyn help Carolyn up the stairs and into Carolyn's bedroom. Jessi smiled as she looked around the room. She'd forgotten, she wrote to me later, about Carolyn's decorating scheme—a shaggy blue rug, and blue-and-white-striped wallpaper. The matching curtains and the bedspread were printed with little black and white cats, and on the bed were two cushions in the shape of cats. Jessi even saw a cat wastepaper basket with pointy cat ears and a furry tail. But one thing in the room didn't belong there. It was a camp bed, next to Carolyn's bed.

"What's the camp bed for?" Jessi asked.

"That's where *I've* been sleeping," said Marilyn. "My room's too far away from Carolyn's. I want to be sure I'm here if she needs me in the night."

Jessi nodded. She was beginning to

understand. Marilyn had been one hundred per cent serious when she said she'd never leave her sister's side. What was amazing to Jessi was how well Carolyn seemed to be taking her twin's protectiveness. Jessi wrote to me that she would have gone crazy if someone had been hovering over her all the time. But Carolyn seemed perfectly content to be waited on every minute and to have her twin nearby all day.

"So, tell me about your science project," Jessi said to Carolyn. Marilyn walked to Carolyn's desk, picked up a small light bulb, and started to explain to Jessi how her sister was making a tiny generator set.

"Aren't you supposed to do science projects on your own?" Jessi asked Carolyn. "I mean, without help?"

Carolyn nodded. "She's not really helping me," she said. "I know much more about science than she does, anyway. But when I need a part or something she gets it for me."

"Well, how about if we leave you to work for a while?" Jessi said. "Marilyn needs to practise for her piano lesson."

"No way!" said Marilyn. "I'll do that later, when Carolyn can be downstairs, too. I can wait while she does her stuff."

Jessi rolled her eyes. "Marilyn, haven't you got homework, too?" she asked. "How about if you bring it in here?" Her suggestion seemed to please Marilyn, and before long the twins were elbow-to-elbow at Carolyn's desk, working quietly together. The girls didn't have much space, but they looked happy.

After about an hour, Carolyn said that she needed an extra part for her generator and that she couldn't do anything else until she had it. "I've finished *my* work, too," said Marilyn.

"Great," said Jessi. She'd been sitting quietly in a corner of Carolyn's room, reading a Mrs Piggle-Wiggle book she'd taken from the shelf. "I suppose we could go downstairs, then, and Marilyn can practise."

They made their way down the stairs (with Marilyn sticking close to Carolyn in case she needed help), and Marilyn hurried to arrange a chair and cushions for Carolyn next to the piano bench. Carolyn made herself comfortable in the chair, and Marilyn fetched her a book to read. Then, at last she settled down to practise.

Marilyn's very good at piano—she's been taking lessons since she was four—and according to Jessi, the next half an hour was very pleasant. She and Carolyn sat and read while Marilyn played through the pieces she was working on for her lesson.

Afterwards, they decided to play a game of Go Fish. As she picked up her cards, Jessi found herself wondering how Marilyn managed to take care of Carolyn all day at school. There was no way she could be near her every second during a school day. At last, Jessi's curiosity got the better of her, and she asked, "Marilyn, how do you take care of Carolyn at school?"

Marilyn giggled. "I try to stay near her as much as I can," she said. "But when I can't be with her, Gozzie takes care of her."

"Gozzie?" repeated Jessi.

"Gozzie Kunka," said Marilyn. "She's a good friend of mine."

That was when Jessi remembered that Gozzie Kunka was an imaginary friend that Marilyn had made up once when the twins weren't getting on very well. She smiled at Marilyn. "That's great," she said. "I bet Gozzie does a good job."

Carolyn nodded, smiling. "She's fun," she said. "But I like Marilyn better."

Jessi could see that, Gozzie Kunka or no Gozzie Kunka, Marilyn was going to stick pretty close to Carolyn for quite a while.

9th
CHAPTER

Saturday

Dear Mallory,
   How are you feeling? You must be tired of being sick. It's too bad ME has to last so long. Do you miss babysitting? Are your brothers and sisters taking good care of you and bringing you bon-bons to eat while you lie around reading all day? I wish you could visit me here and lie in the sun — it would probably make you feel a lot better. Then again, things are pretty exciting here lately, and

the action might be too much for you. You won't believe what happened at the beach today...

I wrote that letter to Mallory when I got back home from the beach on Saturday evening. It had been a beautiful day, sunny and warm. I'd spent the morning working at the beach programme with Sunny. The kids had just about worn us out, and when the programme ended we practically collapsed, glad we'd decided to spend the rest of the afternoon just relaxing. We arranged our things in a good spot in the sand with our blankets laid out neatly and our flasks of juice close by. Then we sat back and watched the waves for a while.

"Hey, you two!" said Jill, from behind us. She and Maggie were floundering through the sand, weighed down with blankets and beach bags. Jill's sister Liz had driven them to the beach to meet us, and the plan was for Liz to pick us up at the end of the day and drive us home.

"We've brought some great munchies," said Maggie, putting her bag down next to me.

"We could stay here for a week, with all this food," said Jill, laughing. "Maggie's made sandwiches, and I've made oatmeal biscuits. We've brought loads of fruit too."

I realized I was starving, and I think Sunny was, too. We helped ourselves to sandwiches and offered our juice to Maggie and Jill. For a while, nobody said a word. We were too busy eating.

"How come you two aren't surfing today?" asked Jill, when she'd finished the last bite of her sandwich.

"We decided to take a day off," Sunny answered. "The waves seem rather high." We looked out at the waves. They *were* high, but plenty of surfers were out. The really good surfers love riding those screamers. As I mentioned before, they use extra-large boards, called guns, when the waves are big. Actually, some surfers call those boards rhino-chasers. Great name, isn't it? I think surfing slang's almost as much fun as surfing itself.

"The contest is still on, isn't it?" asked Maggie. "I heard a rumour that it was going to be cancelled." Maggie and Jill like horseriding more than surfing, but they pay attention to a good surfing rumour when they hear one.

"No way!" said Sunny. "It's definitely on."

"But some people are dropping out," I added. "They think the contest is jinxed or something. Because of Thrash disappearing."

"Not just that," said Sunny. "What

about all the accidents?"

There had been several minor accidents in the past week or so. A couple of surfers had been hurt, but neither of them badly. Some people said it was just coincidence. Others claimed that the ghost of Thrash was responsible, that he was haunting the beach and trying to ruin the contest. Guess which theory *I* believed? Right. I was still convinced that Thrash would haunt the beach till his murderer was exposed and justice was done. But I didn't know how to find out who the murderer was.

"Look at Paul!" cried Sunny suddenly, pointing towards the waves. "He's really carving that breaker!"

Carving, in case you're wondering, means surfing very well. And a breaker's a wave, of course. I watched Paul surf towards the shore. He did look good. He and Carter had been practising non-stop for the competition, and I had a feeling he might do well.

I leaned back and studied the surfers for a while, enjoying the sight. The more you know about surfing, the more fun it is to watch. After all the lessons I'd had and all the practising I'd done, I could appreciate how hard just standing up on a surfboard is, let alone looking cool doing it. And I was really impressed by the moves some of the guys could do. It was as if they understood the waves, and could use each one to do exactly what they wanted. They had perfect balance, and could make the boards turn through the waves so they looked as if they were cutting through butter. And at the ends of their rides, most of them executed this great move called a kick-out, a quick, short turn in which you step to the back of the surfboard and get off the wave. It looks incredibly cool.

Of course, *I'm* more likely to take a nosedive with my board at the end of a ride, and fall headfirst into the water! I'm sure everybody who sees me surf knows I'm a grommet. That's what experienced surfers call *in*experienced surfers. I try not to let it bother me. After all, everybody has to start somewhere. Every surfer was a grommet once.

I picked up a handful of sand and let it trickle through my fingers. I thought about Thrash, and how even he had once been a grommet. After a lot of practice and hard work, he'd become one of the best surfers around. And now he was gone. It didn't seem right. I turned away from the waves and picked up a book of ghost stories Sunny had lent me. It looked like a good one, full of creaky staircases and skeleton hands. I settled down to read for a while.

Jill had brought a pile of magazines, and

she and Maggie were leafing through them. Sunny was trying out a new shade of nail polish, putting it on her toes before she applied it to her fingers. We were pretty quiet for an hour or so.

"Hey, where did everybody go?" Sunny asked suddenly. "The beach has really emptied."

I looked up. She was right—hardly anyone was on the beach except for us. The surfers had left, and not many people were sitting or strolling on the sand. "The fog's coming in," I said, peering out to sea. "I suppose that's why they left early."

"It's rather creepy," said Jill. "I wish Liz were coming back for us sooner."

"I don't think it's creepy," said Maggie. "I like fog. It's like a big blanket covering the beach."

I didn't say anything, but I agreed with Jill. I was beginning to feel spooked. It was about four-thirty, and the sun was starting to go down as the fog rolled in. "Perhaps we should start packing up," I said. "We could wait for Liz in the car park."

"Good idea," agreed Sunny. "It's getting a bit chilly out here." I could tell she didn't want to admit to being spooked any more than I did. She stood up and started to shake out her blanket. I began to throw things into my beach bag, making sure I didn't forget anything. If you leave a hairbrush or a trainer on the beach, it's hard to find.

Jill was folding up her blanket and Maggie was brushing the sand off her feet. I was just tucking the ghost story book into my bag when I heard Sunny gasp. "There's still a surfer out there!" she said. "I don't believe it. It's almost dark!"

"The surfer ghost," I whispered, peering at the waves. "It must be him."

"I can't see anybody," said Jill, squinting.

"Right there," said Sunny, pointing.

"All the way out there?" replied Maggie. "But that's so far out. I can hardly see."

We strained our eyes, trying to catch sight of the surfer. "He's a bit closer now," said Sunny. "I can see him better. And I don't think it's Thrash, Dawn—or Thrash's ghost. He's got pretty short hair, for one thing."

"He's coming in towards the old pier!" cried Maggie. "Let's run down there and see if we can get a better look."

We dropped our things on the sand and started to run, keeping an eye on the surfer. "Whoa!" said Sunny, all of a sudden. She stopped short. "Did you see that?"

"What?" I asked.

"That guy just did an aerial. A three-sixty!"

"Wow!" I exclaimed. Aerial manoeuvres are really hard. You perform them when your surfboard's up in the air while you're turning. And a three-sixty is the hardest turn to make, because you spin all the way round until you're facing the direction in which you started.

"Nobody on this beach can surf like that," said Sunny slowly. "In fact, I've only seen one person do that move." She gave me a serious look. "Thrash," she said. "I saw Thrash do that about a month ago."

Jill and Maggie were staring at Sunny, and so was I. "You mean—" I started to say.

"I mean, short hair or not, that surfer *must* be Thrash. Or Thrash's ghost. I still don't think there's any such thing as a real ghost, but I know I saw *something* strange out there."

"Well, we've lost him now, whoever he is," spoke up Jill. "I can't see him any more." She looked again at the waves, and shook her head. "Anyway, we should get moving if we're going to meet Liz on time."

It was nearly dark as we walked back to our spot and picked up our stuff. Jill and Maggie grabbed their things and walked on ahead, but Sunny and I lagged behind, still glancing at the waves. "You know," said

Sunny. "Whether or not that was an actual ghost, I'm beginning to think there *is* something fishy going on at the beach. I'm going to help you investigate. From now on, we're a team."

I stuck out my hand, and we shook on it. "All right, partner," I said.

On the way to the car park, we passed the food kiosk. It was almost closing time, and the workers were clearing up. A couple of them were kids I know, and I waved. Then I noticed a new guy. He had short black hair and a deep tan, and I know this sounds silly, but he gave me the creeps. I stared at him for a second, and then I looked away and dashed after my friends. Within minutes, we were piling into Liz's old banger. I was surprised at how relieved I felt as we drove off. I was glad to be safe in a car, heading away from the beach on that foggy, dark night.

10th CHAPTER

Wednesday

Dear Shannon,

I sure wish you and the other BSC members could be here to help me solve this mystery. I can't seem to get anywhere with it! I haven't found any new clues in days, and meanwhile things are getting dangerous on the beach. I always thought of the beach as a safe and beautiful place, but lately I'm not so sure about that...

Around the time I wrote that letter to Shannon, I was feeling pretty frustrated with my mystery. The can of wax had been the last clue, and finding that seemed like a long time ago. Sunny was helping me now, and I was glad to have her company, but even with two of us working we didn't seem to be getting anywhere. I'd gone back to my surfing lessons, but Sunny and I made time to talk to people on the beach every day, hoping to find someone who had witnessed Thrash's fatal accident. Nobody had seen anything. We checked with the police on a regular basis. The only thing that happened was that they got sick of seeing us walk into the station. And we combed the beach, looking for any sign of Thrash, but we never found a thing.

Sometimes I felt ready to give up, but Sunny would persuade me that we needed to continue working. Other times, Sunny would say there was no point in trying to solve the mystery, but I would talk her into one more round of questions or one more walk down the beach.

What really kept us going was our sense that the beach was becoming a dangerous place. I don't know if it was because Thrash's ghost was wreaking vengeance (lots of people talked about that) or if it was just coincidence, but in the week or so after Sunny, Jill, Maggie and I saw the surfer ghost, there were a lot of accidents on the beach. And they didn't just happen to surfers.

For example, one day at the children's programme, the kids were playing Simon Says. Dean was Simon, and he was doing all kinds of funny things. The kids were giggling as they tried to keep up with him. "Simon says rub your tummy with one hand while you pat the top of your head with the other," Dean would say. "Simon says try to kiss your elbow." Then he'd catch them out by saying, "Do the moon walk," while he demonstrated a perfect move. Before long, only four kids were left. Ruby, the girl who travels on our bus, was one of them.

"Simon says walk like a penguin," said Dean, showing them how to waddle along in the sand. Suddenly, I heard a shriek that sounded serious. Ruby sat down on the sand, holding her left foot and wailing like a fire engine. I rushed to her side.

"What's happened?" I asked, reaching for her foot. I saw a ragged cut in it, and a small amount of blood. Luckily, the cut wasn't deep, but it looked as if it must hurt a lot.

"I stood on something," sobbed Ruby. "Something awful!"

While Alyssa cleaned and bandaged the cut, Sunny and I combed the sand where she'd been penguin-walking. We couldn't find anything that might have cut Ruby's foot.

The next day, Ruby was back in high spirits. She said her foot hardly hurt at all, and that her mum had given her chocolate pudding as a special treat the night before. That day, everything went smoothly at the children's programme. But after our surfing lesson, when Sunny and I were packing up to leave the beach, we heard sirens. We ran to the parking area to see what had happened, and found a small fire engine and an ambulance pulled up by the food kiosk.

"What's happened?" Sunny asked one of the workers.

"Freak accident," said the boy. "The grill flared up all of a sudden and burned Brenda's eyebrows right off! Luckily, she wasn't hurt apart from that. The ambulance men have just checked her, and she's fine."

We saw the firemen examining the grill and shaking their heads as if they couldn't work out what was wrong with it. And, as far as we heard in the days after the accident, they never *could* explain the flare-up.

A couple of days later, a man returned to the car park to get his car and found that all four tyres had gone flat, for no apparent reason. Another man said he'd been dive-bombed by an angry seagull. And a woman was stung by a jellyfish while she was walking in the shallow water at the edge of the beach.

Sunny and I tried to make light of each incident, but even though nobody had been seriously hurt, we were scared. Why were all these things happening at once? I mean, I knew that these accidents could happen at any beach, but all in the space of a week? It was really weird. We took extra care when we watched the kids at the beach pro-gramme, making sure none of them went unsupervised for even a few minutes. And Sunny and I stuck together like glue. "I'll watch out for you if you'll watch out for me," she joked.

I felt most nervous while I was surfing. I still loved it, and I looked forward to my lessons. But accidents were happening to surfers, too. In fact, there had been at least one accident every day for a while. As I've said, surfing *can* be a dangerous sport, and there's always the potential for trouble when you're out in the water. Waves aren't entirely predictable, and even the best surfers can make bad judgements.

But bad judgement didn't seem to be the problem. Bad *luck* did—and lots of good surfers were having it. Paul was hurt when he fell off his board and it was carried towards him by a wave. It hit him on the shoulder, and since then his arm has been in a sling.

Wanda fell off her board and was underwater for so long she almost drowned. And somebody else collided with the old pilings where the pier used to be. Rosemary was caught in the riptide (that's a strong current that moves away from shore) and the lifeguards had to go after her in their rubber boat.

TJ fell off when his board didn't respond the way it should have during a turn he was trying to make. Then the same thing happened to somebody else. And that's when the rumours started.

"No way were the waves that gnarly," said Carter one day when Sunny and I were making our usual rounds, talking to the surfers. "I mean, those dudes can handle massive screamers, and those rollers weren't anywhere near overhead."

"So what are you saying?" asked Sunny.

"I'm saying that somebody messed with their boards. Just like somebody messed with Paul's leash."

"What?" I said. I hadn't heard anything about Paul's leash. (A leash is a cord that connects at one end to a surfboard and at the other to a band around the surfer's ankle. It keeps the board from getting lost, and sometimes helps to guard against the board hitting the surfer if he falls off.)

"It's the truth, man," said Carter. "Everybody's talking about it. They're saying that some wack wants to win that competition really badly. So badly he doesn't care if another dude gets hurt. So badly he might mess with a board. Some of the dudes are getting pretty nervous about it. I heard Spanky's dropped out of the competition."

"He *did*?" I asked. I was surprised. Spanky's a great surfer, and everybody thought he'd do well in the competition.

"Yes," replied Carter. "I mean, Thrash is history, right? Spanky isn't interested in getting killed, too. So he's going down to Mexico for a while, to surf where he won't get hurt."

The rumours kept flying, and the accidents kept happening. But Sunny and I continued to surf. You might think we were crazy, but we weren't ready to give up our new sport. Besides, the *good*, experienced surfers were getting hurt, not the grommets like us. We were no threat in the competition. Therefore, nobody was going to try to get rid of us. Right? Well, the theory made sense to us. Anyway, Buck said we were really coming along, and that if we stopped practising now we'd never improve.

Then, one afternoon (it was the day after I wrote that letter to Shannon, as a matter of fact), something terrible happened. Sunny and I had just finished our lesson, and we were standing on the beach with our surfboards. "I'm exhausted," I said. "Ready to start packing up?"

"In a few minutes," said Sunny. "I want to go out one more time. Look at those waves! They're perfect." She had a point. It had been a great afternoon, and the waves were still rolling in regularly, looking green and glassy. They were just the right height, too. Five or six people were paddling out on their boards, getting ready to ride back in.

"You're right," I agreed. For a second, I thought about going back in with Sunny. But then I felt a wave of tiredness roll over me, and I knew I shouldn't. Buck says it's dangerous to surf when you're not feeling your strongest. "You go ahead," I said. "I'll watch and give you a report on your form."

Sunny grinned. "You'd better give me top marks," she said. She tossed her hair back, grabbed her board, and ran into the water. She put the board down, lay on top of it, and started to paddle out. When she reached the spot where the other surfers were waiting, she turned and watched the rollers coming in. In turn, each of the surfers caught one. It's bad surfing manners to take somebody else's wave, so Sunny waited patiently until everybody else was already riding in. Then she got ready for the next wave. When it came, she turned her board towards the shore, and as the wave rushed along, she climbed on to it and began to ride.

"Looking good!" I called, even though I knew there was no way she could hear me over the booming surf. Sunny stood with her arms out, balancing carefully. Even from a distance, I could tell she had a big smile on her face.

And then, Sunny disappeared. "Oh, my lord!" I cried, as soon as I saw that she was down. I ran to the edge of the water and scanned the waves, waiting for her head to pop up. It seemed like hours until I saw first her board, and then her head and shoulders, riding in towards the shore on a gentle wave. I ran to meet her and helped her out of the water and on to the sand. She was gasping for breath and coughing.

"Are you okay?" I asked. "What happened?"

"Don't know," she said, still coughing. "I think the nose went under."

I knew just what she was talking about. Once the nose goes under the water, there's almost no way to keep from falling off your board.

"My elbow's killing me," said Sunny. "And my shoulder, too. I really got thrown around."

By that time a crowd had gathered, and one of the lifeguards was checking Sunny for broken bones. "Looks like you'll survive," he said, "but you'd better head for the hospital and get a proper examination."

Sunny spent that night in hospital. She was badly bruised, and the doctors wanted to keep her in for observation. Her mother rang me the next morning and told me she'd asked Sunny to give up surfing, at least for a few weeks. "But that means she can't be in the competition," I said.

"That's right," replied her mother. "And she's very disappointed about it. But she asked me to tell you not to give up. And she said not to give up on "the other thing", either. Whatever that means."

I didn't tell Mrs Winslow, but I knew exactly what Sunny meant. "The other thing" was our mystery, of course. Now it was more important than ever to get to the bottom of it.

11th CHAPTER

Saturday

Dear Dawn,

Your mystery sounds so cool! I wish
I could be there to help you to investigate (and maybe get in some surfing,
too!). Meanwhile, back in Stoneybrook,
things haven't changed too much.
Except for one thing. I know you've
heard about the Arnold twins and
what they're going through. Well, things
got even worse before they got better.
But I think Marilyn and Carolyn are
on the right track now...

That was only part of a long letter that Stacey sent me, explaining the Marilyn-and-Carolyn situation in detail. During the week before she wrote to me, she sat for them three times. On Sunday, she was at their house in the afternoon. Mr and Mrs Arnold had gone to the christening of a friend's baby, leaving the twins with strict instructions about their chores. They were both to clean their rooms, Marilyn was supposed to load the dishwasher and Carolyn was supposed to dust the furniture in the living room.

Stacey was glad to see that Carolyn was feeling a lot better. Her ankle had healed, and she didn't have to wear the support bandage any more. Her crutches were propped by the front door, waiting for Mr Arnold to take them back to the hospital the next day. Stacey was relieved. She thought the twins would be back to normal, and that Marilyn would feel all right about letting Carolyn out of her sight. But Stacey was wrong. Marilyn was still taking her promise very seriously. The twins were inseparable.

Stacey had hoped that she and the twins could have some fun once the girls finished their chores, but their chores took up the whole afternoon. Why? Because neither of them could or would do anything alone. Marilyn had to watch while Carolyn vacuumed her room. Marilyn made sure Carolyn was close by while *she* cleaned *her* room. (Which wasn't very messy, as Marilyn was still sleeping in her sister's room.) After that, they both made for the kitchen, where Carolyn hovered around while Marilyn loaded the dishwasher. Then they went to the living room, and Marilyn watched Carolyn dust. Stacey was exasperated to say the least.

On Tuesday, Stacey met the twins after school and spent the afternoon with them. They were both doing gymnastics in the basement again, now that Carolyn was well. But they were being very careful. Very, *very* careful. Marilyn watched every single step that Carolyn took, even when she wasn't doing anything dangerous. And Carolyn was equally zealous about watching Marilyn. "It was like ultra-ultra spotting," Stacey wrote to me. "I mean, Carolyn couldn't *breathe* without Marilyn trying to help her. Ridiculous!"

On Thursday, Stacey saw the same pattern. The twins were never out of each other's sight. They were driving Stacey crazy, and she knew she had to do something about it. But what? She had another job booked at the Arnolds' on Saturday afternoon, and she was dying to work something out before then. At last, at Friday's BSC meeting, she told the others what was happening.

"It can't be healthy for them to be together all the time like that," said Mary Anne. "I mean, especially as they're twins. They need their separate identities."

"I know," replied Stacey. "That's exactly the problem. And I've got a feeling that Mr and Mrs Arnold think so, too. They seem rather impatient with the twins."

"They'd probably be grateful if we could help," mused Kristy.

My friends thought about the problem for a while, but nobody came up with any suggestions. And then the phone began to ring, and they were busy arranging jobs.

By the time the phone stopped ringing, it was almost six o'clock. "Phew!" said Shannon, ringing off after the last call. "We're booked solid for the next week."

Mary Anne looked at the record book. "No kidding," she said. "If anybody else phones we're going to have a problem. I mean, every single one of us has a job tomorrow afternoon!"

Stacey had been deep in thought while the others were booking jobs. But Mary Anne's comment seemed to wake her up. "That's it!" she cried. She grabbed a pencil and a piece of paper from Claudia's desk. "Okay, who's sitting where tomorrow afternoon?"

"I'll be at the Pikes'," said Kristy. "Mal and I will be sitting together. We're going to do quiet, indoor activities." That was the deal the Pikes had made with Mal. While she was recovering from ME, she could sit for her own brothers and sisters with another club member, as long as she stayed indoors.

"Great," said Stacey, scribbling notes.

"I've got a job at the Papadakises'," said Shannon.

Claudia was taking Charlotte Johanssen to the art museum, and Mary Anne would be taking Logan's brother and sister to watch one of his basketball games.

"I'll be at the Braddocks'," added Jessi. "But why are you asking?"

"I've got a plan!" said Stacey, her eyes gleaming. "Are you ready for this?" She leaned forward and told them her idea.

The next day, Stacey headed for the Arnolds', feeling much more optimistic. She was almost positive that her plan would work.

Mrs Arnold answered the door when Stacey knocked. "Oh, I'm glad to see you!" she said. "I could do with a break from the twins." She laughed and shook her head. "I know it's just a phase, but I hope they'll get over it soon."

"I know what you mean," replied Stacey.

"The girls are downstairs," said Mrs Arnold. "They're working on a new gymnastics routine in which they can perform at the same time. They call it 'twin-nastics'."

Stacey laughed. "Great name," she said. "Perhaps it'll be an Olympic event one day."

"Hi, you two!" she said, as she ran down the stairs.

"Hi, Stacey!" said Marilyn.

"Want to see our new routine?" asked Carolyn.

"Okay," said Stacey. She sat on the bottom step and watched as they performed. As she explained in her letter, they'd worked out their routine very neatly. One twin would be on the balancing beam, for example, and the other would be spotting her but also performing similar moves, on the floor. "Looks great, girls," said Stacey, "What does your gymnastics teacher think of it?"

"She hasn't seen it yet," said Carolyn.

"We've just started working on it," explained Marilyn. "But I'm—*we're*—sure she'll like it."

Stacey nodded. The girls returned to their practising, and Stacey played audience. Now and then she glanced at her watch. At precisely two o'clock, the phone rang. "This is it!" Stacey said under her breath. She ran upstairs to answer it. It was

Kristy, as she'd known it would be. The plan was in motion.

"Hi, Stacey!" said Kristy. "I'm at the Pikes', and I've brought over the new Flying Horses tape. Margo wants to know if Marilyn would like to hear it, too."

Good. Kristy was sticking to the script. "Hold on," said Stacey. "I'll get Marilyn." She called down the stairs, and both girls came running up.

Marilyn took the phone. "Hello?" she said. Kristy had put Margo on the other end, and Margo repeated her invitation. Marilyn listened, and broke into a smile. "I'd *love* to hear it," she said. Then she caught herself. "I mean—if *Carolyn* can come, too." She listened again, and frowned. Then she looked up at Stacey. "Margo's only allowed to invite one person over today," she said.

"So? You can go by yourself."

Marilyn shook her head. "No, I can't," she said reluctantly. "Sorry, Margo, but I can't come." She rang off and shrugged. "Oh, well," she said. She and Carolyn went back to the basement.

Stacey followed them, checking her watch again. At exactly two-fifteen, the phone rang again. This time, it was Jessi, calling from the Braddocks'. Haley wanted Carolyn to come and play with her new video game. When Carolyn got on the phone, a grin spread across her face. "Princess Power?" she squealed. "I've been *dying* to play that!" She paused. "Can Marilyn come, too?"

Haley said the game was meant for only two players. Carolyn looked hopefully at Marilyn, but Marilyn shook her head, and Carolyn had to say no to Haley.

The girls trudged back to the basement, downcast. Stacey stood in the kitchen, timing them. Exactly seven minutes later, Marilyn and Carolyn pounded back up the stairs.

"We've changed our minds!" exclaimed Carolyn.

"We decided it was okay to be apart— for a couple of hours, anyway," said Marilyn.

Carolyn rang Haley, and Marilyn rang Margo, and soon they were ready to go. The girls decided they would all walk to the Pikes' first, and then Stacey and Carolyn would continue to the Braddocks'. Stacey left Mrs Arnold a note, explaining where they'd gone, and then they were off.

Stacey smiled to herself as she and the twins walked down the road. "I knew it was only a little step," she wrote to me that night, "but it *was* a step. That's good enough for me."

12th CHAPTER

Thursday

Dear Mary Anne,

Stacey wrote me about the latest development with the Arnold twins. Reading her letter sure made me miss the BSC. The We ♥ Kids Club is great, but they're not quite as involved with their clients as the BSC is. I miss those meetings when we would sit around and talk, talk, talk about what was going on with the kids.

Meanwhile, things are really heating up around here. Today I got my first big break in the mystery. Here's how it happened...

I wrote that letter to Mary Anne one night after a long—and exciting—afternoon at the beach. I was there for the kids' programme, but I wasn't working with Sunny or Alyssa. I had a special job: a one-to-one sitting job with Stephie Robertson. You see, the beach programme was involved in rehearsing a play to be put on for the parents. It was a special production of *Alice in Wonderland*, which Alyssa and Sondra had adapted so that it took place on a beach. It was called *Alice at the Beach*, and the kids were having a great time with it. But Stephie's really shy. She didn't want to be in the play, and Alyssa didn't want to force her. Instead, Alyssa had arranged for Stephie to be my responsibility during rehearsal times.

We'd been enjoying our time together, Stephie and I. She's a great kid. In fact, she reminds me more than a little of Mary Anne, and it's not just because they're both so shy. It's also because, like Mary Anne, Stephie's an only child. And she's growing up without a mother, just the way Mary Anne did. Stephie's mum died when Stephie was just a baby. Her dad's bringing her up, and I know he tries hard, just as Mary Anne's dad always did, but it's not always easy for a man to bring up a daughter by himself. He has help—a nannie lives with them—but I can tell Stephie misses having a mum. She doesn't talk about it, but I can just tell anyway, maybe because I'm so close to Mary Anne.

Anyway, Stephie and I had found plenty to do. We went for long walks, exploring parts of the beach we'd never been to before. We watched the surfers, and rated their form. And we spent a lot of time collecting pebbles, beach glass and shells.

Stephie's dad had given her a nature guide to beaches, and we'd been working our way through it. We'd identified all the birds we saw, and most of the shells we picked up. We'd even learned a lot about different kinds of seaweed! Those afternoons with Stephie were great. The time I spent with her was relaxing, and I needed to relax. Most of the time I was caught up in trying to solve the mystery of Thrash's disappearance, but when I was with Stephie I managed to put that aside. Instead of thinking about mutilated surfboards and phantom surfers, I concentrated on being a friend to Stephie.

That Thursday, the day I wrote the letter to Mary Anne, Stephie and I had been busy categorizing the pebbles we'd collected. We'd made different piles for green stones, black stones, stones with stripes, white stones—well, you get the picture. There was even a pile for heart-shaped stones, which were Stephie's favourites. I liked the flat stones best, the ones you could use for skimming stones.

We'd also spent some time reading to each other. Stephie loves books, and she's an excellent reader. I bet she'd get on really well with Charlotte Johanssen. Stephie's been working her way through the Narnia books, and we were in the middle of *The Silver Chair* that day. As Stephie read, I lay back in the sand and watched the waves roll in. A lot of surfers were out that afternoon; the competition was the following weekend, and everybody was getting in their practice time.

When Stephie finished her chapter, I stretched and sat up. "I'm hungry," I said. "How about you?"

"I'm starving," she replied, smiling.

"Let's go and get smoothies," I suggested. Smoothies are blended fruit drinks made with yoghurt, and they're delicious. My favourite kind is banana-strawberry. The kiosk on the beach makes them with tons of fresh fruit.

"Great!" said Stephie. "I want a peach one today."

We packed up our things and headed for the kiosk. On the way, Stephie and I waved to Sunny and some of the kids in the beach programme, who were rehearsing a scene in which Alice meets the surfing Cheshire Cat.

"They look as if they're having a good time," I said to Stephie. I wondered if she felt left out.

"I'm having a good time, too," she said, taking my hand and looking up at me with a smile.

The kiosk was crowded with people waiting to order chips, hot dogs and smoothies. Stephie and I got into the queue, and I craned my neck, curious to see who was working that day. A girl called Shari was working the blender, but none of the other people looked familiar. Then I saw him. That new guy, the one with the black hair. The one who'd given me the creeps the first time I saw him. He *still* gave me the creeps, but I couldn't work out why. He was working the grill, flipping burgers a mile a minute. As the queue we stood in edged forward, I stared hard at the guy, trying to work it out. He wasn't being rude to the customers, or staring at girls or anything. He was just doing his job.

The closer I moved to the counter, the better I could see him. He was dressed like the other workers, in cut-offs and a T-shirt. His hair was very short. He must have got the haircut recently, too, because his neck wasn't as tanned as the rest of him. Unlike the rest of the workers, who were wearing wild jewellery, he wasn't wearing any. I did notice, though, that he had holes in his ears for pierced earrings. Two in the left, and three in the right. I counted.

He was wearing dark, dark sunglasses, the kind that wrap around your head and make you look like some kind of space ranger. And as he turned to place a burger on a bun, I noticed a funny white mark on his finger. A scar? I tried to get a closer look, but just then I realized that the girl behind the counter was talking to me. It was my turn to be served, and Shari was waiting for me.

"Hey, Dawn," she said. "I bet you're here for a smoothie. Strawberry-banana, right?"

I nodded. "Right," I said. "I suppose I'm pretty predictable."

"Oh, we just get to know all the regular orders," she said. "Anything else?"

I ordered a peach smoothie for Stephie, and we watched while Shari blended our drinks for us.

"Yum!" said Stephie, as Shari dumped sliced peaches into the blender. Her drink was ready first, and she started sipping it while Shari prepared mine.

"Okay?" asked Shari, putting my drink on the counter. I nodded, and handed her some money. As she was sorting out my change, I glanced once more at the creepy guy. Suddenly, I realized something incredible. Something so crazy, I could hardly believe it. "Dawn?" asked Shari, holding out my change. "What's the matter? You look as if you've seen a ghost or something."

I tried to laugh. "I'm okay," I said. I took the change, grabbed my smoothie, and thanked her. "Let's go, Stephie," I said.

We left the kiosk and walked towards the car park, as it was almost time to catch the bus home. "What's happened?" asked Stephie. "You look upset."

"It's nothing," I said. I wasn't ready to tell *anybody* what I'd worked out. Stephie and I sipped our smoothies while we waited for the bus. I could hardly taste mine, but I pretended it was delicious. I chatted with Stephie about our plans for the next day, but I wasn't paying much attention to what she said.

When Sunny met us in the car park, I asked if I could come over to her house after we got home. "I've got something to tell you," I said. "Something about—*you* know."

Her eyes widened, and she gave me a curious look. I shook my head, letting her know that I couldn't talk about it until we were alone. We got on to the bus soon after that, and I felt relieved to sit back in my seat and listen to the kids singing and teasing each other.

When I got home, I ran to my room and dumped my beach stuff. Then I headed for Sunny's. She let me in, and we ran to her room and closed the door.

"You'll never believe who I saw today," I said.

"Who?" she asked.

"It was at the beach kiosk. This new guy there gives me the creeps for some reason. I've tried and tried to work out why, but I couldn't. And then, suddenly, I knew who he was."

"*Who?*" Sunny asked again.

"Thrash."

"You're kidding."

"No. It was him. He looks different, but I know he's Thrash. It's as if he's in disguise." I described the guy to Sunny, and then I explained how I'd worked out he was Thrash. "The mark on his finger tipped me off," I said. "It's a tan line around the ring he used to wear. The one that's shaped like a snake."

"Are you *sure*?" Sunny asked.

I nodded. "He's cut his hair and dyed what's left," I said. "That's why his neck's pale—because his hair used to be longer. And I remember how many holes he had for pierced earrings, because it's one more than I've got."

Sunny looked stunned. "But if he *is* Thrash—" she began.

"He isn't dead," I finished. "But he's still hanging around the beach. Why? What's he up to?"

"This is crazy," said Sunny. "Perhaps we should tell the police."

"No way," I said. "For one thing, they wouldn't believe us, just because this *is* so crazy. And for another, they don't seem to care what's happened to him. I think we've got to check this out on our own."

Before long, I'd talked Sunny into seeing things my way. We spent half an hour planning what to do next, and then I went home for dinner. My head was spinning. Thrash wasn't dead, after all. He was very much alive. Alive and well and working— undercover—at the beach kiosk.

13th CHAPTER

Friday

Dear Claudia,
   The mystery of the surfer ghost just keeps growing. Mary Anne probably told you how I learned that Thrash is still alive. Once I discovered that, all I had to do was find out what he was doing hanging around the beach in disguise. This mystery sure is keeping me busy!

"Look at that, Sunny," I whispered, nudging her. It was the day after I'd spotted Thrash, and Sunny and I had wasted no time putting our plan into action. We'd finished at the beach programme, and raced to the beach kiosk to see if Thrash would be there again. I saw him straight away. He was cutting up lettuce for sandwiches, and he seemed to be concentrating hard on his work. I took the opportunity to point him out to Sunny.

"No way!" she whispered. "Are you *sure* that's him?"

Just then, Thrash turned towards the counter, and Sunny got a good look at him. He was still wearing sunglasses, but I knew she was checking out his pierced-ear-ring holes and the strange tan line on his finger. "Hmmm," she said. "You know, I think you're right. But what's he doing *here*?"

"That's what we have to find out," I whispered. I walked up to the counter and ordered us a smoothie each. We watched Thrash carefully while we were waiting to be served, and then we walked down the beach, sipping our drinks. We decided to watch Thrash as much as possible and try to work out what he was up to. As Sunny still couldn't surf, she could spy on him while I had my lessons and practised. And as I was still sitting for Stephie during the hours of the beach programme, I would try to hang around the kiosk and watch him then.

Over the next few days, we spied all the time. One or the other of us kept an eye on Thrash whenever we were at the beach. But we didn't find out much. Basically, all he did was work. I have to admit that Sunny and I were both feeling frustrated.

Meanwhile, I was practising hard for the surfing competition. I was even having trouble concentrating on my schoolwork, because I was so intent on the competition. Buck said he was proud of my progress, and that I was turning into a "radical surfer". I knew he was exaggerating to make me feel more confident, but I knew I really *was* improving. Some days I felt so in tune with the waves that it seemed I'd been born in the water. I knew I wouldn't win any top prizes in the competition, but I was looking forward to it anyway.

There were still reports, now and then, of sightings of the surfer ghost. As Sunny and I were never at the beach after dark, we didn't see him. But everybody was talking about the amazing moves the ghost could pull. They joked about the ghost entering the competition, saying he could probably win first prize if he did.

Sunny and I checked with the police a couple of times, but they had no new leads on the case. They still thought Thrash was either dead or missing, and they weren't exactly hot on the trail. In fact, they seemed to have written him off and moved on to other things.

The day of the competition grew closer and closer. All the surfers were practising hard, and some were riding the waves from early morning until the sun went down. Certain surfers were beginning to look discouraged, and others were wearing this confident, almost cocky look. There was a lot of talk on the beach about who would win which prize. Surfers like Gonzo and TJ seemed to regard each other suspiciously. They checked out each other's form and copied moves they thought might catch the judges' eyes. Even with Spanky gone, there were plenty of really excellent surfers getting ready to compete.

On Saturday, the day before the competition, Alyssa asked Sunny to stay for an extra half-hour after the beach programme finished. Sunny had agreed weeks ago to help with the sets for the play when the time came, and now, said Alyssa, the time had come. I was on my own until my lesson started, so of course I made my way to the beach kiosk to check up on Thrash. Guess what? He wasn't there. I went up to the counter and ordered a smoothie. When the girl who made it handed it over, I spoke up. "Hey, where's that other guy who usually works here?" I asked casually. "You know, the one with the short hair."

The girl shrugged. "I think he asked for the day off. Why?"

I thought fast. "Oh, he lent me fifteen cents the other day when I didn't have enough change," I said, trying to sound convincing. "I wanted to pay him back."

She nodded. "He'll probably be here tomorrow," she said. "Anyway, it's only fifteen cents. I doubt he's worried about it."

I agreed. As I walked away from the stand, I racked my brains. Where could Thrash be? And why had he taken the day off? I had a feeling that something was going on. I suppose it was what TV detectives call a hunch. Somehow I knew it was important that Thrash had taken time off work on the day before the surfing competition.

I walked past the surf shop, deep in thought. As I rounded the corner of the building, I heard a strange noise. I drew back and put my smoothie down in the sand. Carefully, I peered around the corner. Behind the shop is a shed where the workers store their surfboards. And somebody was in it. I walked closer, peering into the semi-darkness. That's when I saw Thrash. He was bending over one of the boards and pushing against its fins with some kind of tool.

He was *tampering* with somebody's board!

I drew back again and thought for a second. What Thrash was doing was wrong, and somebody had to stop him. If he messed up that board, its owner could get seriously hurt. I looked around, hoping to see a policeman—or *anybody* who could help. But nobody was there. It was up to me. I took a deep breath and gathered up my courage. Then I walked into the shed, clearing my throat as I approached Thrash.

"Hey!" I said, trying to sound official. Unfortunately, all that came out was a squeak. Thrash didn't pause in what he was doing. He didn't look up, either. "Hey," I said, more loudly. "What do you think you're doing?"

All of a sudden I wondered if I was crazy. Was this guy really Thrash? Or was he somebody else, somebody who might be really angry about being caught tampering with a board? Somebody who might try to hurt me.

This time, he did look up. But he didn't seem angry or upset. He just grinned at me. "Hey, Kelea," he said. "How's it goin'?"

That's when I knew for certain he was Thrash. He's the only person who's ever called me by that name. "Thrash?" I said, uncertainly.

"That's me."

"So you aren't dead."

"No. Alive and kicking."

"And tampering with somebody's board," I said. "That's not right."

"Hey, somebody tried to off me," he replied, defensively. "You know, kill me. Make sure I wasn't in the competition. I know who did it, too. Well, I fell pretty badly after he messed with my board, but I didn't die. I let him think I did, though. I want to teach that jerk a lesson."

"What do you mean?"

"Why do you think I'm still hanging around?" he asked. "And why do you think I look like this?" He put down the tool and ran a hand through his short black hair. "I *hated* to cut my hair, man, but it was the only way. I thought if I disguised myself, I could still hang around here. I could keep surfing, and prepare for the competition. I could still win it, too, and make some money so I can head Down Under, to Australia."

"But I suppose you're not so sure you can win honestly," I said, "seeing as you're messing up that board."

He glared at me. "I'd win no matter what. But I want to teach this guy a lesson. Nobody messes with Thrash."

"What if he gets hurt?" I asked.

He shrugged. "Not my problem. I mean,

121

that dude wasn't worried about *me* getting hurt, was he?"

"Have you been messing with other people's boards?" I asked. "I mean, there have been all these accidents, and—"

"I'm not responsible," Thrash said, holding up his hand as if he were swearing to it. "This is the only one I care about. I just want to get my own back on that guy for what he did to me."

I decided to change the subject while I thought about what to do next. I had to prevent Thrash from tampering with that board. "You said you've been surfing, but I've never seen you out there."

"Never seen the Surfer Ghost?" he said, grinning.

"You mean—?" I began. My mouth dropped open.

He nodded. "That's me. I've been riding the waves by moonlight, just to make sure nobody tries to spy on me and steal my moves." He laughed. "It's a riot how they all think I'm a spook," he added.

"I saw you," I said. "You really did look like a ghost out there."

"Cool." He picked up his tool again and bent over the board.

"Don't do it," I said. "Please. I mean, I understand that you want revenge, but two wrongs don't make a right." I didn't *mean* to sound like a teacher; the words just popped out. "And anyway, you said you could win the competition without messing up that guy's board. I think you should enter the competition honestly, under your own name. That way, you can prove to everyone that you really are the best surfer."

Thrash gave me a long look. "Yeah, but if I just turn up alive, the guy who messed up my board is going to get away with it. What about that?"

"There has to be a way to make sure he gets into trouble for what he did," I said. "Let me think for a second." I leaned against a saw-horse.

Thrash stood there looking at me. "You're too much, Kelea," he said. "Why do you want to help a bum like me, anyway?"

I didn't know how to answer him, because it was a mystery to me, too. But there was something I liked about Thrash. He was a terrific surfer, and I knew he deserved a chance to win that competition fair and square. And I knew that the guy who had messed with his board deserved some kind of punishment for what he'd done. Just then, I had a great idea. I smiled at him. "I don't know *why*, Thrash," I said. "But I think I know *how*."

14th
CHAPTER

Sunday

Dear Kristy,
   Wow! How can I begin to
tell you about everything
that happened today? I'm
totally exhausted, and totally
stuffed with artichokes and
vegetarian lasagne (Dad
took us out to dinner after
the contest) but I'll try to
stay awake long enough to
write down the main events
of the day. So, let's see. First
of all, I woke up late...

"Oh, no!" I sat bolt upright in bed that morning, staring at the clock. I was going to have to hurry if I wanted to get to the beach on time. Then my glance fell on a pink sheet of paper Buck had handed me the day before, after my last lesson. "Preparation for Competition", it said at the top. It listed the things you should do before a contest, and at the top of the list was, "Be sure to get plenty of rest the night before you compete." Well, I'd definitely done that!

I jumped up and started to gather my stuff together. As I was throwing things into my beach bag, I heard a soft knock on the door. "Sunshine?" asked Dad, coming into my room. "Feeling okay? Ready to show the judges your stuff?"

I grinned. "As ready as I'll ever be. That is, if I can get there on time."

"Don't worry about *that*," he said. "I'll get you there. Carol arrived ten minutes ago, and she and Jeff are ready to leave whenever you are." He gave me a big hug. "We're so excited about watching you compete," he said.

"Oh, Dad. Really, I'm not very good yet. I hope you're not expecting too much."

He just hugged me again. "Come on down when you're ready," he said.

When I got downstairs, they were waiting

for me: Dad, Carol and Jeff. "Let's go!" I said.

Carol handed me a bagel from the breakfast table. "You can't compete on an empty stomach," she said with a smile.

"Thanks," I replied, thinking that Carol had been pretty easy to get along with lately. She was right, too. "Make sure you eat something" was the *second* item on Buck's list. I didn't feel hungry at all—I was jittery and excited. But I took a bite of the bagel anyway, and brought it and an orange with me to the car.

We piled in, Jeff sitting beside me in the back seat, and soon we were on our way. As we drove, Dad kept up a steady stream of talk about what a perfect day it was for the contest, and how crowded the beach would be for the big event. I just sat, looking out of the window, thinking about everything I'd learned from Buck. I thought about how to choose the right wave, and how to sense the moment to climb up and ride it. I reviewed my best rides, picturing the things I'd done right. "Positive visualization," Buck calls it. He says the pros do it. In the middle of one of my "rides", I felt Jeff's elbow digging into my side.

"This is for you," he said. "For today. I'm lending it to you, for good luck." He handed me a penny. "I found it in school one day," he said. "And I kept it. It's a lucky penny."

"Thanks, Jeff," I said, putting my arm around him and giving him a squeeze. "I'll put it in my wetsuit pocket." I tucked it away. Then I looked out of the window again. We were nearing the beach, and I started to think about Thrash, wondering what he would do about competing. He had told me, at the end of our talk, that he was going to go to the police and tell them everything he knew about the guy who'd tampered with his board. I was glad, as that was the plan I'd come up with. But beyond that, I had no idea what he was doing. For all I knew, he wouldn't show up at the competition. The police might even have put him in prison when he confessed to trying to tamper with the guy's board. Or maybe they'd just told him to clear out, leave town. I might never see Thrash again.

Still, I was betting that he'd turn up at the competition. Thrash loved being the best surfer on the beach. I didn't think he'd pass up the opportunity to prove it to everyone.

"Wow, it's a mob scene!" said Jeff, when we arrived at the beach. "*Everybody's* here."

He was right. The beach was packed with surfers, fans and judges. Everybody was milling around, waiting for the contest to begin. The waves looked great—smooth and glassy and not too big. *That* was a relief. I'd been worried about having to deal with huge grinders or choppy seas.

Everyone wished me luck, and I made my way towards the group of surfers who were gathering near the judges' stand. On the way, I ran into Sunny, who had come to watch the contest even though she couldn't take part. "Good luck!" she said. "And have fun. I'll see you afterwards, okay?"

I pointed her in the direction of Dad and Carol and Jeff, and she said she'd join them. Then I ran to the judges' stand to check in. As I was giving my name, I heard a murmur run through the crowd of surfers. I looked up just in time to see Thrash stroll to the stand.

He was blond again—I suppose he'd dyed his hair back—and he was wearing his earrings and the snake ring. He looked as much like his old self as he possibly could. He was even carrying a surfboard like his old one, with black designs on a purple background. I heard a few gasps as he walked through the crowd.

"I'm back from the dead," he announced, with a cocky grin. "And ready to rock and roll."

I heard a strangled scream from behind me, and I turned to see Gonzo drop his surfboard in the sand. Gonzo! I should have known. He had turned completely pale, and he was staring at Thrash as if he were seeing—you've guessed it—a ghost. Then he turned, and ran down the beach.

"That's him!" yelled Thrash. "Get him!"

Suddenly, several men in the crowd, men I hadn't recognized, took off down the beach after Gonzo. They were dressed like surfers, but as soon as they started to chase the guy, I knew—I just *knew*—they were undercover policemen.

Sure enough, after they'd caught up with Gonzo they pulled badges out of their shorts pockets. Gonzo immediately confessed to tampering with Thrash's board, and the police took him away. It turned out that the police had talked Thrash into working with them, which was exactly what I'd hoped they'd do. I knew if he felt the police were on his side, he would be more likely to enter the competition honestly.

It took a while for things to calm down, but before long the judges were announcing the start of the competition. The first group to compete would be the beginners. That was me. Suddenly, I felt like running back to Dad and climbing into his lap.

"Go for it, Kelea!" said Thrash from behind me. "You can do it."

I smiled at him. "Thanks," I said. "I'll do my best."

The male beginners went first. I watched as one after the other chose bad waves and fell, or took short, unimpressive rides. I started to feel a bit better. I might be a beginner, but I was sure I could do better than *that*. I watched the waves carefully, trying to decide which ones I would pick if I were out there.

At last the men's division finished and the women's began. There were five of us. We paddled out and began to eye the waves more closely. I was supposed to go second. My stomach was in a knot, but I could also feel a certain kind of energy that I knew would help me through my rides.

Contest scoring is based on a lot of things. The length of the ride, for one. The longer you can ride, the more moves you can catch, and the better you look. Another factor is manoeuvres, or moves. The judges watch to see how smoothly you do certain things, and whether you take chances on exciting, radical moves. You also get judged on style, and on how well you choose your waves.

As I waited for my turn, I tried again to visualize the perfect ride. When the first surfer finished her ride (a very short one), I waited patiently until a wave I liked came along. Then I rode it in, trying hard to remember everything Buck had told me. It wasn't a bad ride.

Each of us in the division had three turns. My second ride was terrible: I fell off my board almost right in front of the judges' stand. But I stood up and shook the water out of my hair and paddled back out. My third ride was one of the best I've ever had.

When my division had finished, all I could do was watch the other surfers and wait to find out the results. The judges wouldn't announce the winners until the whole competition was over, and at first I didn't know how I could stand the wait. But before long it was the turn of the experts, and I got involved watching the really good surfers do their stuff. Spanky had turned up at the last minute, so the competition was fierce. Wanda, wearing a wild purple wetsuit, looked great in the women's division.

Boy, did those surfers have some radical moves! They carved up the waves, making turns that looked impossible. And Thrash was obviously better than anyone. My respect for him grew as I watched him. He was calm and in control, and he looked completely happy out there in the surf.

At the end of the day, a huge group of very tired surfers gathered around the judges' table to hear the results. Dad, Carol, Jeff and Sunny had joined me, and I think they were even more nervous than I was about who would win in the women's beginners division.

The judges announced the men's beginners first. Then it was time for my division. "First prize," said one of the judges, "goes to Katie Bear." Sunny glanced at me with sympathy, but I shrugged. No way had I expected to win *any* prize, much less first. But guess what? I won *third*! And let me tell you, walking up there to accept that yellow ribbon was one of the proudest moments of my life.

There was no doubt in my mind—or anyone's probably—that Thrash would win the overall prize for best surfer. And sure enough, he did. He didn't get a ribbon, though. Instead, he got a big fat cheque. He held it up and waved it over his head. "See you all Down Under!" he shouted, grinning. He gave me a special wink, and I winked back.

What a day! I was exhausted—and starving. That night, Dad took us out to dinner at my favourite vegetarian restaurant. I ate all of my dinner and some of Sunny's too. Later, as we were driving home, I gave Jeff back his lucky penny. "Thanks a lot," I said. "It definitely worked!"

15th CHAPTER

Monday

Dear Mum,
   I miss you! I wish you
could be here with me.
Sorry I haven't written
much lately, but I've been
really busy. I helped to
solve this incredible mystery-
but I'll tell you more about
that next time we talk.
And guess what? I won
a prize in the surfing contest!
I'm enclosing the ribbon I
won. I'd like you to have it
for a while. At least until
I'm back in Stoneybrook,
that is!

Love you
   —Dawn

I decided it was safe to write to my mum, now that the mystery had been solved and the contest was over. If I'd sent her the kinds of bulletins I'd been sending my friends over the past few weeks, she would have been worrying her head off. I would probably never tell her *all* the details of the mystery, but now I could share some of it with her.

Life was pretty much back to normal. I was studying hard for a maths test at school. Sunny and I were still busy with the beach programme. She was surfing again, carefully, and I surfed with her. I was rather relieved that the competition was over, so we could just surf for fun and not worry about practising.

I hadn't seen Thrash since the contest, and I decided he must have already left for Australia. And of course, nobody had seen the surfer ghost since the contest. As I said, life was back to normal.

On Friday evening, the kids at the beach programme put on their play. Stephie and I sat in the audience and applauded wildly for the actors. The parents loved the play, and the kids seemed to have a great time acting it out, especially Erick, who made a terrific Mad Hatter. Alyssa and Sondra had done a great job with the script and the costumes, and Sunny's sets were perfect.

The next day, I was finishing at the beach

programme when I spotted a familiar figure walking along the beach with a surfboard. Thrash. He was still around, after all. I waved to him, and he waved back. Then, to my surprise, he ran up to me. "Hey, Kelea!" he said. "Congratulations! You did really well in the competition."

"So did you," I said. "You were awesome."

"Thanks. And, hey—thanks for your help. I was definitely on the wrong track, messing with that guy's board. You put me straight. I wouldn't let too many people talk to me the way you did, but I'm glad you were there."

I smiled. "Wasn't it better to win fair and square?"

He laughed. "Definitely."

"So, I thought you were heading for Australia," I said.

"I am. I'm leaving tomorrow. In a few days, I'll be hitting the surf Down Under. Maybe you'll get there, too, one day. You'd like it, Kelea." He smiled at me. "You know, I'm a bit of a loner. I've never been used to having friends. But I think you were my friend, and I think I learned something from that. I wanted to thank you." He paused. Then he did something that really surprised me. He pulled the snake ring off his finger and handed it to me. "I want you to have this, to remember me by." He tossed it to me.

"Wow!" I said. The ring felt heavy in my hand. I tried it on, but it was much too big for any of my fingers. "I'll put it on a chain and wear it round my neck," I said. "Thanks, Thrash. I won't forget you."

"Cool," he said. "Well—later!" He turned and loped off. I watched him go, knowing I would never again meet anyone quite like him.

That night at home, I found a chain to put the ring on. Standing in front of the mirror, I hung the chain around my neck. The ring looked special and mysterious, and I knew I would treasure it.

On Monday I came straight home from school and headed for the phone. I dialled Claudia's number, knowing it was a meeting day, and my friends would be gathered in her room.

"Babysitters Club!" said Kristy, answering the phone.

"Hello," I said, trying to sound ultra grown-up. "This is Mrs Heidendorferman. I'd like to book a sitter for my triplets, Larry, Moe and Curly."

"Hi, Dawn!" said Kristy, cracking up. It's hard to fool her, but it's easy to make her laugh.

"How *are* you all?" I said. "You can't believe how much I miss you!"

"We're fine, and we miss you, too. The meeting's just breaking up, so you can talk to everybody, if you want."

"I want to, I want to!" I said. Dad had agreed to let me make this phone call after I promised to do some extra chores. I was determined to get my money's worth.

"Congratulations on solving the mystery," said Kristy. "And *double* congratulations on winning the contest. We knew you could do it!"

I heard clapping in the background, and my friends' voices calling, "Yea, Dawn!"

"So," said Kristy. "How's the We ♥ Kids Club? Is business good?"

"Very good," I said. I told her about a picnic we were planning.

In the background, I heard Claudia say, "Kristy, come on! Let *us* talk to her."

"Did you hear that?" Kristy asked. "I suppose I'd better hand the phone around. See you!"

Stacey grabbed the phone next. "Hi, Dawn!" she said. "So tell me, was this guy Thrash cute or what?"

"He was, I suppose. But he wasn't really my type. Too old, for one thing." Stacey's so boy-crazy sometimes. "But there are a lot of cute guys on the beach," I added. "And they all ask about you. They say,

'Hey, where's that friend of yours from Connecticut?'"

"They do *not*," said Stacey, giggling. "How would anybody remember me?"

"Just kidding," I said. "Too bad you couldn't be in the contest, Stace. I bet you would have won something."

"I don't know about that," she said. "But we're so proud that *you* did. Anyway, I'd better go. Claud's about to tear the phone out of my hand!" I heard a shriek, and then Claudia was on the line.

I talked to her for a couple of minutes, and then the phone was passed to Shannon, and then to Jessi. It was so great to hear their voices. I asked Jessi how Mal was doing, and she said she thought it wouldn't be too long before she was back to normal.

At last Mary Anne got on the phone. "Hi, sis!" she said. "How's the California ghostbuster?"

"I'm great! How are you? How's Tigger? How's Logan?"

"Everybody's fine. Your mum hung the ribbon you won over the fireplace. She's so proud of you."

"What else is going on?" I asked. I was hungry for news from Stoneybrook.

"Not much. Just the same old things, really."

I heard somebody shout in the background, "Tell her about the Arnold twins!"

Mary Anne laughed. "Did you hear that?" she asked. "I can't believe nobody's told you yet."

"What happened?" I asked. "Are they still sticking together like glue?"

"Not exactly," said Mary Anne. "Get this: they had a big fight, and now they aren't speaking to each other!"

I cracked up. "After all that!" I said. "What was the fight about?"

"Neither of them even remembers. But they each swear the other one started it."

"Of course," I said. Just then, Dad came into the room, pointed at his watch, and raised his eyebrows. "Er, Mary Anne," I said. "I think I'd better go. Dad's giving me the signal."

"Okay," she said. "It was great to talk to you. I miss you, sis!"

"I miss you, too. You and everyone in the BSC. But I'll be back in a few months."

"I can't wait."

"Neither can I," I said, feeling rather sad all of a sudden. It was hard to be so far away from my friends and my stepsister. "'Bye!"

After I rang off, I pottered around my room for a bit, thinking. I smiled to myself when I remembered what Mary Anne had told me about Marilyn and Carolyn. I knew they wouldn't stay angry with each other for long. They were too close. After all, they're best friends as well as twins.

I glanced down at the ring Thrash had given me. It hung on the chain round my neck, reminding me of him. I hoped Thrash would have a best friend one day, so he could find out how great friendship can be.

Friendship. There's nothing like it. Getting to know a loner like Thrash has made me even more grateful for the friends I've got, both in Stoneybrook and in California. They're friends I'll *always* have, no matter where I live. That makes me a really lucky person!